Jakeera Mckendrick

"A Mother's Love Gone Wrong"

by Jakeera Mckendrick

This is a work of fiction. Names, characters, Business's, places, events and incidents are either the products of the Authors imagination or used in a fictitious manner. Any resemblance to actual person's living or dead or actual events is purely coincidental.

Appreciation

Many of you have been waiting for Part 2 for almost a year and have been writing me trying to figure out when I would be dropping it. I always said soon because I was battling with myself and my own personal growth I didn't feel like it was good enough. After re reading Part 1 numerous of times I finally decided that it had to be re written and instead of making you wait for two new books I combined them both so we all get what we want. Which is how we ended up here, this book is monumental and it needed to be written better but I had to grow personally and mentally for that to happen which is what took so long. Thank God for his grace because without him I would have never noticed that this book could have been better so God I thank you for showing up and getting me together when I didn't even know I needed it. Thank you to all of my supporters, you guys made AMLGW a success when it wasn't its best so I'm excited to see the reaction to this version. Thank you to my family and friends for always pushing and motivating me. I have to give a special shout out to my dad man because he helped me grow so much mentally and help aide me in abandoning a lot of my ugly ways so Mr. Beatle I appreciate you, my guy for life! Thank again to everyone who believes in me and loves my writing this is for you! God bless

Present Day

"How did you feel about the workshop today?" Amora asked her student Sierra as they sat in one of their weekly mentoring sessions. Instead of responding, Sierra shrugged her shoulders and remained quiet.

"Did it help you think about what it is you want to do about your future?" Amora inquired.

"No! and no offense Ms. Amora but for a girl like me that has been from group home to group home. Listening to those women talk about how they had family to help to them and parents to guide them I honestly couldn't relate at all" Sierra replied honestly.

"It didn't motivate you not even a little bit? I know if I was in your shoes I would have took that as motivation. Because although my current situation in these different group homes may not be what I want right now, I know better is obtainable if I apply myself the right way." Amora expressed.

"How can you tell me how to feel? Better yet how can you tell me how to take anything? Do you live and walk in my shoes every day? Ms. Amora my life is real! I go through real shit every day. Every day is a struggle to survive, I don't have anybody at home pushing me and explaining shit to me. Everything I'm learning is on my own. And you know what I'm starting to realize about life" Sierra asked her.

"What's that?" Amora replied.

"That bad shit happens to good people and the bad people are blessed with good shit" Sierra told her as tears fell from her eyes.

"That's not true Sierra! Life happens to everyone, not just you! We all have different paths in life that we have to go through in order to be who God called us to be" Amora explained to her.

"I don't believe in God" Sierra replied.

"May I ask why?" Amora asked.

"Because if God was real, he would have protected me from all of the hurt and abuse I've encountered over the years. I used to pray, a lot actually but when I noticed that he never answered any of my prayers and he just let all of this bad shit happen to me I came to the conclusion that he just isn't real. And life is about surviving on your own" Sierra told her wiping her tears with the sleeve of the hoodie she was wearing.

"What do your tears represent right now?" Amora asked her.

"Anger" Sierra chuckled. "My life is pretty messed up! I wonder what it would feel like to talk to someone that can say you know what Sierra I know exactly how you feel because I went through it! Now let me tell you how it can get better because it did for me" She continued. "You sit up here and talk to us about our futures and becoming better then you bring these women in here to tell us the same thing. You want us to listen to these success stories coming from people with real families and parents that raised and cared about them but in all honestly it goes in one ear and out of the other. We don't have that so we don't comprehend how being successful is "obtainable" as you say because you didn't have to overcome what we have to" She finished.

"Well I never told you I had parents to guide me nor did I tell you that I had a perfect life" Amora told her.

"You didn't have to, it's obvious! You're super pretty, intelligent, have multiple businesses and a shit load of money! I know you had parents that helped send you off to college and get you all set up for life" Sierra replied.

"A shit load of money? Where you get that from?" Amora laughed.

"We see that Bentley you're pushing Ms. Amora they cost a grip! Unless it's really your nigga who has the bread and he brought everything for you." Sierra suggested.

"What if I told you that it's neither one of your assumptions" Amora told her.

"I would say you are lying and that's no disrespect to you" Sierra expressed.

"Have I ever lied to you before?" Amora asked her.

"No well not to my knowledge" Sierra replied.

"I haven't, but I see I made the mistake of not allowing you girls to get to know me! I expected you all to listen and relate to my current life, never acknowledging that it's my past that you really need to know about" Amora told her as she sat in deep thought. She never considered telling her story to anyone because it's a past she fought to overcome and forget about. However the purpose of her organization "B.E.A.T'N ME" is to help provide an environment and guidance for young girls to see that success is possible but it's starts with them. At 26 years old Amora runs a Non - Profit organization where she mentors young girls in bad neighborhoods and provide them with the tools and necessities needed to become powerful female who know the importance of envisioning the highest version of themselves then consistently competing against that person.

"What about your past? Ms. Amora if you didn't experience true hurt and abuse, I'm talking about foster father raping you while your scary ass foster mother sat in the next room pretending not to hear type of hurt. We can't relate! If you didn't overcome some real life stuff don't waste your breathe and my time because there is no comparison." Sierra yelled with emotion.

"When you hear about the "real shit" I've not only encountered but survived, I don't want any more excuses out of you Sierra! I'm about to show you that it's never good to judge a book by its cover. When I was 15 my mother, myself and my younger sister Sionni all moved from King of Prussia which was considered the "suburbs" to West Philly which is basically the hood. Yes my parents were married and we lived under the same roof for a nice amount of my life but my parents didn't love each other and that affected my sister and I more than they could imagine. Once my parents divorced my father went about his life and we stayed with my mother" Amora began her story.

11 years ago…

"Amora just stack all of the boxes in the living room neatly and I'll sort them through them later" My mother Stephanie instructed leaning on the hood of her car as an all black Mercedes Benz pulled alongside us.

"Just moving in?" The driver asked.

"Yeah as you can see" She replied with sass.

"Need any help?" He offered.

"No we have it covered! Thanks for offering though." She told him.

"No problem! I always make it my business to help others, especially when they are as pretty as you." The driver flirted.

"Oh is that so?" My mother flirted back once she got a good look at him.

"Very much so." He replied stepping out of the car. "I'm Damien by the way, what's your name pretty lady?" He asked.

"Stephanie! It's nice to meet you Damien." She replied.

"I would love to get to know you, if that's okay with you." He told her.

"That's fine with me, let me put my number in your phone!" She said, before taking his phone and storing her number in it.

"Excuse me mom, can I take a break, I'm tired." I asked out of breath interrupting their conversation.

"Yeah go head Amora," She replied dismissively.

"She's beautiful! Is she your only child?" Damien asked.

"No, I have one more." My mother told him.

"Oh okay. You're blessed because she is beyond beautiful," Damien said as he looked back at me as I took a seat on the front steps.

"Thanks." She replied dryly.

"Well I would love to stay and talk to you but I have to get to service. I will be calling you later on tonight," Damien told her.

"Service?" My mother questioned.

"Yes. I'm a Pastor, my church is about 15 minutes from here." He told her.

"Oh okay! Maybe I'll come by one day" She replied.

"You will eventually," He replied confidently and pulled off. I sat on the steps wondering who this stranger was talking to my mother, not even realizing that the stranger I was staring at was the devil himself and would be the cause of majority of the hardships I was about to endure. Two months after meeting my mother was stuck on Damien like white on rice and obsessed with everything about him. Damien insisted on meeting my sister and I, so my mother set up a formal introduction between us.

"Amora if I call you again and tell you and your sister to come on we're going to have a problem!" My mother yelled into the phone as soon as I picked it up.

"Okay Mom, we're coming out now." I replied before hanging up. "Sionni come on now! I don't feel like her today" I screamed at my younger sister.

"I'm coming dang, Amora you don't have to yell at me," Sionni pouted.

"I'm sorry Sionni, I just don't feel like her stuff today. She's already fussing and I just don't feel like hearing her mouth." I explained. I had to soften my tone with Sionni because she was extremely sensitive and would cry in a heartbeat the moment someone yelled at her. At 15 years old, I was practically raising my 8-year-old sister on my own. Yeah we lived with my mother, but she wasn't exactly the ideal mother figure. Stephanie wasn't your average 40-year-old; she didn't look nor act her age. She was 5'8, light brown complexion with almond shaped brown eyes, solid 185 lbs. with shoulder length jet black hair, thick hips and tiny 32B breasts. When she wasn't chasing behind one of her many boyfriends, she was out trying to find a new one. All my mother was concerned with was money and men.

"About damn time; Amora you're going to make me put my hands on you! I told you to have both of yall ready by the time I got here and you still took your time!" My mother yelled at me as soon as I got in the car.

"I'm sorry mom!" I replied. I knew that if I said anything else my mother would not hesitate to punch me in my face like she had done on plenty occasions. As my mother continued to rant, I turned my head and stared out the window wishing this wasn't the life I had to live. Ever since my father divorced and left my mother, she took her frustrations out on me. Sionni however, was her weak spot, but because I reminded her so much of my father I felt like she despised me.

"Now I want the both of you to be on your best behavior. Amora watch your mouth and those sarcastic ass remarks." My mother scolded my sister and I as we pulled up to the church and parked.

"Yes, ma'am!" We replied in unison as the three of us got out the car and walked into the church.

"Hello everyone!" My mother greeted the four church members sitting in the sanctuary.

"Hello Stephanie" The women spoke to my mother dryly. "Hey pretty girls!" They continued greeting Sionni and I with a smile pissing my mother off. She grabbed Sionni's hand and yelled for me to follow her as she led us to the Pastors office and knocked.

"Come in!" He yelled out.

"Hey you," My mother smiled and sashayed over to him giving him a kiss on the lips before sitting on his lap.

"Hey yourself," He replied kissing her back and looking over at Sionni and I.

"Well well well, I finally get to meet the two beauties that have captivated the hearts of all of my church members." Damien said before removing my mother from his lap and walking over to us. Damien wasn't a bad looking guy, he stood at 6'2 with a dark chocolate complexion, 210 lbs. He had a muscular build, bald head, white pearly teeth and round light brown eyes. That was probably the reason why my mother was so crazy over him; he may take the cake for being the best looking guy she has dated, outside of our father.

"Hello beautiful, I'm Damien and you are?" He asked as he grabbed my hand.

"Amora, and this is my sister Sionni." I replied with my head down. I wasn't sure what was going on, but being in Pastor's Damien's presence made me feel very uncomfortable especially from the way that he was staring at me and caressing my hand. Snatching my hand away, I stood up and walked over to my mother.

"I have to use the bathroom," I whispered to my mother causing her to grip me by my shirt and yank me closer to her.

"If you don't want to get your feelings hurt, I suggest you go sit back down." She threatened. Not really wanting to go sit back next to Damien, I stood there in her face hoping

12

she would pay attention to the fact that I was completely uncomfortable.

"Amora don't test me," She warned before pushing me back over towards the couch Sionni and Damien were sitting on. Hearing what my mother said to and noticing the weird look on my face, Sionni spoke up.

"Umm mommy, I have to use the bathroom." She said sweetly. Already knowing how we operated, my mother rolled her eyes before telling me to walk Sionni to the restroom.

"Thanks Sionni,"I sighed once we were inside of the bathroom.

"Don't thank me, I saw how you started acting funny when he grabbed your hand and I heard what mommy said to you. I knew she wasn't going to get like that with me so I had to say something," Sionni replied while rubbing my back. I sat on the toilet and put my head down. Trying to fight back the tears that were forming in my eyes, I let out a huge sigh.

 "Ugh Si I just don't feel right about him, he is very weird and just keeps touching me." I told her.

"I know Amora. I think he likes you and its making mommy mad." Sionni added.

"What do you know about a boy liking a girl?" I asked her.

"Nothing, but I know he was acting the same way mommy other boyfriends act with you and he called you beautiful like them, so he must like you like them too!" Sionni replied. My mother did not only dislike me because of my father but also because of how beautiful I was. Everywhere we went, I got so much attention, even from the many men she juggled, they all would rant about how beautiful I was and it pissed my mother off. She gave me many black eyes, several broken arms and plenty of bruises in attempt to lower my self-esteem so that when I received the many compliments I would shy away and not think too highly of myself and it worked! I was very insecure to be so pretty. Unlike my younger sister I looked nothing like her mother, but was the spitting image of my father. Standing at 5'1, light brown skin complexion with almond shaped grey eyes and dark naturally curly hair that fell to the middle of her back, I was beyond beautiful and I was young and still had room for development. I had the perfect body to match my blemish free face with my slim waist, flat stomach, round ass and perky 32C breast that sat up perfectly. Although I was very thankful for my looks I couldn't help but wish I didn't have the face and body I had. I felt that maybe if I wasn't so pretty my mother would love me and treat me how she treated my sister.

"Don't remind me Sionni! That's why I wanted to get out of there." I replied with tears running down my face.

"Don't cry sister it will be okay! I know it hurts your feelings the way she treats you, but you know I love you and I got your back no matter what. Plus, when I get a little bigger like you and she try to punch on you we can jump her!" Sionni joked in an attempt to make me smile.

She hated the way my mother treated me but there wasn't much she could do besides give me the love my mother didn't. Sionni loved me and would always tell me how beautiful she thought I was. She despised my mother at times for making me feel like my looks were more of curse than a blessing.

"Si you so silly," I said as I stood up and wiped my face.

"I love to see you smile," She said before hugging me. "I love you Amora." She told me.

"I love you more Sionni. Now let's get back to your mother before she come in here and drag us out of here." I said before grabbing my sister's hand and walking out of the bathroom. As we left the bathroom we bumped right into one of the woman who attended the church.

"Oh my god I'm sorry! We didn't expect anyone to be standing here," I apologized.

"It's okay beautiful. You okay? You look like you've been crying." She asked once me she noticed how puffy my face was.

"Yes I'm okay! I just have allergies." I lied quickly.

"Allergies huh? Well alright then!" She replied. "You know sometimes when we are upset, it's okay to talk about what's bothering us with someone who cares and is willing to listen." She explained to me. "My name is Joseline, but you can call me Sister Joseline. Whenever you want to tell me what's bothering you I promise I will be here to listen." She explained with sincerity.

"Thank you Sister Joseline, I will remember that," I told her before hearing my mother walk out of Pastor Damien's office. My mother stopped in her tracks once she noticed who we were talking too then cut her eye at me before mustering up the fakest smile she could find and speaking to sister Joseline.

"Hello Sister Joseline, how are you?" My mother asked her.

"Hi Stephanie, I'm good and yourself" Sister Joseline spoke back dryly. At the time I didn't understand what their beef was but as time went on everything began to make sense.

"Couldn't be better." My mother replied while rolling her eyes and turning her attention to my sister and I.

"What took ya'll so long?" She asked.

"My stomach was hurting and I had to take a poop mommy," Sionni spoke up.

"Eww Si too much information." My mother said laughing. "Come on stinky!" She joked. "Let's go Amora!" She turned serious and said to me. Walking behind my mother and sister, I couldn't help but feel sad all over again. All I wanted was for my mother to show me the same kind of love and attention she showered my sister with. I couldn't understand why my mother was punishing and treating me the way that she did. It was emotionally, mentally and physically draining for me and I honestly was growing tired of the verbal and physical abuse I was forced to endure on a daily basis.

"It was nice meeting you two beautiful ladies today," Damien spoke when we walked back into the office.

"Nice to meet you too," Sionni responded while I remained quiet and smiled.

"I look forward to spending more time with you two." He smiled while looking at me.

"Stephanie make it your business to call me later. I have another appointment coming in a few minutes that I need to get ready for." He spoke while standing up and walking over to the couch where Sionni and I were seated. He kneeled down and shook Sionni's hand before turning his attention to me. "Hopefully next time you won't be so mean to me beautiful." Damien said before grabbing my hand and kissing it. Snatching my hand away from him and standing to my feet, I looked at my mother who had fire in her eyes and walked out of the office. I knew what was coming next and was sure my mother was about to do a number on me just by the look in her eyes.

Hearing Pastor's Damien office door open then close, I didn't even bother to turn around, I knew it was my mother and sister walking out. Brushing past me, my mother held Sionni's hand while walking back through the sanctuary and saying her goodbyes to the members of the church. Before I could walk out of the door sister Joseline grabbed my hand and stopped me.

"Remember what I said beautiful, I'm here to listen whenever you're ready to release whatever is bothering you." She spoke while squeezing my hand.

"Thank you, I will remember that," I smiled and said.

"Let's go Amora!" My mother yelled when she noticed I had stopped and was talking to Sister Joseline again.

"I'm sorry, I have to go," I said snatching my hand then running and catching up with my mother and sister.

"Why do you keep talking to her?" My mother yelled at me once we reached the car.

"She stopped me and was talking to me mom I didn't go to her." I tried to explain to her.

"I DON'T CARE STAY AWAY FROM HER DO YOU HEAR ME?" She yelled before unlocking the car doors.

"*Yes I understand!*" I mumbled with my head down and climbed in the back seat.

"No get in the front seat. We're not done!" She screamed. Already knowing what was about to happen, I mentally prepared myself as I climbed out the car and got in the front seat. Closing the door, I reached over my shoulder and put my seat belt on, before I could turn back around my head hit the passenger seat window.

"Didn't I tell you not to go in there and embarrass me?" My mother yelled as she forcefully grabbed a handful of my hair and banged my head into the window repeatedly.

"Mom I didn't do anything! What did I do?" I cried while trying to block the impact of my head from hitting the window.

'You think I didn't see how Damien was acting towards you? I'm sick of you every time I turn around somebody calling you beautiful and shit. He is my man he isn't supposed to be showing you more attention than me. Caressing your hand and stuff what type of mess is that!" My mother ranted as she rained constant blows to my face.

"Mom please stop she's bleeding. Amora didn't do anything why are you doing this to her?" Sionni cried from the backseat. It was as if my mother tuned my sister out because she got out the car and walked around to the passenger side. Snatching the door open, she yanked me out of the car by my hair and threw me on the ground before sitting on top of me and punching me repeatedly in the face. Trying my hardest to block the blows, I continued to scream and cry.

"Mom please stop! I didn't do anything please! "I cried.

"Yes you did and I'm going to teach you," My mother said while standing to her feet and kicking me in the face. Feeling myself slip out of conscious, I laid on the ground and balled up.

"Hey hey stop that! What the hell are you doing to that girl?!" A stranger yelled from their window.

"Mind your business nosey ass this is my daughter, I can do what I want to her!" My mother yelled at the old woman watching from her window.

"Amora get up and get in the car now and you better not get any blood on my seats!" She yelled before getting in the car and slamming the door. Struggling to get my balance, I stood up and used my shirt to wipe some of the blood that was pouring from my face. I climbed in the car and cried not just from the pain but because I couldn't understand why this was happening to me. Sionni felt sorry for me because she took off her shirt and used it to wipe off the blood that was coming from my nose. "I'm sorry" She mouthed to me. Shaking my head "No" I turned my head and continued to cry.

Three days after my mother attacked me outside of the church, I was still at home recovering without the help of my mother. I suffered two swollen black eyes, a fractured nose, swollen lip and a huge gash to my head from that beating. Well that's what I diagnosed myself with because she refused to let me go to the hospital. I wasn't able to do too much of anything because of my eyes being so swollen and the excruciating pain my body had been in, so Sionni stepped up to the plate to help nurse me back to health.

"Amora you have to eat something so you can take these medicines I found for you!" Sionni said as she walked into the room.

"What medicines Si? What does the bottle say?" I asked her.

"I don't know how to pronounce it; I just know mommy takes them when she is in pain. It starts with a N. it says N-A-P-R-O-X-E-N," She spelled out.

"Okay. What did you bring me to eat?" I asked.

"I made you a peanut butter and jelly, your favorite!" She replied and smiled.

"Thanks Si. Can you grab me a bottle of water so I can take the medicine when I'm finished this sandwich?" I asked before biting into the sandwich and wincing in pain. Everything on my body was in so much pain, which was why I wanted just to lay down and not move, however I appreciated my sister for caring and attempting to help make me feel better. My mother hadn't been home since the incident happened. I was grateful that I wasn't left alone.

"Here Amora." Sionni said as she walked back into the room with water and ice pack for my head.

"Okay now open the medicine bottle and give me two pills Si," I instructed her.

"I'm twisting it Amora but it's not opening" She whined.

"Push it down some Sionni then twist it. You can do it, don't get upset!" I coached. Doing what she was told, Sionni finally got the bottle of pills open and removed two pills from the bottle then handed them to me.

"Here you go Amora. What else am I supposed to do?" She asked me.

"Put the bottle back in the cabinet and come lay with me. I'm going to take a nap and you can watch TV until I get up," I told her before turning over on my side and getting comfortable. What felt like five minutes later I was being shook out of my sleep.

"Amora! Amora! Wake up!" Sionni yelled while shaking me hard.

"What? What's the matter Sionni?" I asked fully awake.

"I thought you were dead Amora I was so scared, you haven't moved since you fell asleep yesterday" Sionni cried dramatically.

"Omg I was asleep that long?" I asked her, I hadn't realized I was asleep for so long. "I'm going to take a shower Si, I'll be back" I told her climbing out of the bed and walking into the bathroom. Closing the door and standing in front of the mirror for the very first time since my mother attacked me; I couldn't believe my eyes as the tears formed. My once flawless face was covered with black and blue marks and large lumps. Taking a rag and gently washing my face, I winced in pain when the rag touched my eyes. The swelling had finally gone down some so I was able to open them more however the bruising was still bad. After brushing my teeth and taking a much needed shower, I finally re-joined my sister in the room we shared together.

"You okay Amora?" Sionni asked me as soon as I walked into the room.

"Yes, in a little pain but I'll be fine." I told her. "Has mommy been here yet?" I asked as I began to lotion my body.

"Yeah she came in while you were in the shower," Sionni responded. "She said to tell you to get ready for church." Shaking my head, I didn't even bother to respond. It was Sunday, how could I not expect her to finally pop up.

"AMORA!!" My mother yelled from living room. Rolling my eyes, I tightened my towel, walked out my room then down the stairs to see what she wanted.

"Yes?" I responded reaching the bottom step.

"I know Sionni told you what I said. So I'm trying to figure out why you up there dragging your feet and don't have an ounce of clothes on yet?" She scolded.

"I was about to get dressed now mom," I stuttered.

"You have ten minutes to get dressed and get in the car. Think I'm playing if you want to!" She threatened before standing up from the couch and walking out the front door. Rushing up the steps, I grabbed the first thing I could find to throw on just so I could hurry up and get outside to avoid making my mother mad.

"Sionni hurry up and put your shoes on and meet me downstairs," I told her.

"Okay!" She responded doing what she was told. After deciding to just put on a sweat suit, I ran in the bathroom to wet my hair so I could wear it in its natural curly state. Grabbing my bag, I rushed down the steps and out the door while yelling for Sionni to come on. After double checking that I locked up the house, Sionni and I both ran to the car and jumped in. My mother pulled off without uttering a word to either one of us. Fifteen minutes later we were pulling up the church and my sister and I both rolled our eyes while we watched our mother park her car. Before turning the car off she turned around and us.

"Amora if anyone asks you what happened to your face you will tell them you got jumped on your way home from school, understand?" She said to me.

"Yeah" I replied looking out the window.

'Let's see how beautiful these people think you are with your face all messed up like that." She chuckled before turning her attention to my sister. "Baby girl you say the same thing okay? If anyone ask you what happened to your sister you say she got jumped at school alright?" She said to her in a loving voice.

"Yes mommy." Sionni replied.

"Okay now that we have an understanding, let's go and both you be on your best behavior. Oh and Amora stay away from Joseline you understand me?" She scolded.

"Okay mom!" I responded with an attitude evident in my voice. It wasn't that I was trying to be disrespectful but how many times did she think she had to drill that in my head. It wasn't like I initiated the conversations with the people she told me not to talk to, they would always come and talk to me.

"Lose the attitude Amora! That's my only time telling you," She threatened. Not even bothering to respond I got out of the car and waited for my mother and sister to do the same.

"Good morning everyone!" My mother greeted as we made our way through the sanctuary to find our seats.

"Good Morning girls!" Some of the church members greeted. "Morning Stephanie" They greeted dryly. I kept my head down in hopes that no one would notice my face and ask what happened. I hated lying!

"Good morning beautiful!" Sister Joseline spoke walking up behind me.

"Good morning" I replied never bothering to neither turn around nor lift my head.

"Can I get a hug this morning beautiful?" She asked. I looked at my mother for some type of signal of what I was allowed to do but she just simply rolled her eyes and lead Sionni to their seat. Taking that as a go ahead I turned around and gave Sister Joseline a hug.

"Oh My!" She gasped while lifting my face lightly with her hand. "Who in God's name did this to you?" She asked me.

"I got jumped by some girls at school." I lied. I honestly believe she knew I was lying because she looked straight at my mother and shook her head.

"You got jumped huh? Well why would someone want to jump you?" She asked me.

"I don't know, but I have to go." I responded before rushing to my seat.

"What did she say to you?" My mother whispered to me once I sat down.

"She asked me what happened to my face and I told her that I got jumped at school. Then she asked why somebody would want to do that and I said I didn't know and walked away." I told her in one breathe.

"Mmhmm she so damn nosey" My mother cursed "Don't talk to anybody else as a matter fact go sit in the car until service is over." She ordered while reaching in her bag and grabbing her keys then tossing them to me.

"Mom really? Service is always at least two hours what am I supposed to do in the car for that long?" I whined.

"Did I ask you how long service was?" My mother scolded. "Just do what I said and don't stop and talk to anyone on your way out! Now go!" She ordered. Getting up from my seat I walked out of the church completely frustrated! *For all this she could have left me home. What was the point of bringing me when she knew good and well everyone was going to ask what happened to my face."* I mumbled to myself as I got in the car. Putting the key in the ignition I started the car so that I could roll the windows down to get some air.

"Hey there, why are you sitting out here by yourself?" An old woman walking her dog stopped and asked me.

"No reason" I replied before turning my head.

"It has to be a reason because I saw you walk in with two other people but come out here by yourself so tell me why!" The old woman told her.

"You're really nosey you know that?" Amora asked her.

"Me being nosey may help someone one day so I'm fine with that. Now are you going to tell me why you sitting in this hot ass car or not child?" She asked me.

"I told you no reason!" I responded.

"How about you tell me what happened to your face then?" The older woman compromised.

"I got jumped at school" I lied.

"You know what I dislike the most out of everything in this world?" She asked me while scratching the bridge of her nose.

"No what's that?" I replied.

"I dislike when people lie to me. And you child lied straight to my face! I sat up in that window and yelled at your mother for attacking you last week but I'm assuming that is what she told you to tell people huh?" She said with her eye brow raised at me.

"I don't know what you're talking about!" I lied again putting my head down.

"My eyes are up here chile, always look a person in the eyes when you are talking to them. It shows confidence and truth!" She told me as she put her hand under my chin and lift my head up.

"When you're ready to talk I'm here to listen. I'm Mrs. Gionna by the way. What's your name pretty"? She asked me.

"Amora!" I told her.

"Nice to meet you Amora. I live right across the street if you happen to get bored or thirsty from sitting in this hot ass car, you're more than welcomed to come over". Mrs. Gionna offered.

"Okay thank you" I responded. Watching Mrs. Gionna walk away I couldn't help but think how crazy and nosey that old woman was. I didn't understand why everyone I was coming in contact with could tell that I was hiding something and in desperate need to let it out. I didn't trust anybody and I damn sure didn't think anyone could help me so I kept quiet. With nothing else to do I decided to just take a nap until my mother and sister got out of church.

"Amora! Amora! Wake up" Sionni yelled through the window.

"I'm woke Sionni! Stop yelling" I frowned opening my eyes.

"I was calling your name for a while and you wouldn't wake up so I had to yell! But I am leaving with Aunt Sunny, I'm staying at her house for couple days but mommy told her you couldn't come". She told me.

"I knew that was coming!" I replied and put my head back down. My mother didn't allow me to go anywhere, she wanted me where she could see exactly who I was around and who I was talking to. She wanted control over everything concerning me.

"Don't be sad Amora, I'm going to tell daddy to call her and see if she will let you come over tomorrow" Sionni said in an attempt to cheer me up.

"No it's okay Si. Have fun!" I told her before hugging her goodbye. Watching Sionni run over to my aunt's car and get in, I let a few tears fall. I knew why my mother didn't want me to go over my aunt's house, I just wished my aunt cared enough to come and talk to me to see why.

"Hello there beautiful! I missed you in service!" Pastor Damien said as he approached the car breaking me from my thoughts with my mother trailing behind him.

"Hi" I spoke.

"What happened to your face baby girl?" He asked as he put his hand underneath my chin and lifted my head so that he could get a full view of my face.

"I got jumped at school" I replied before snatching my head from his hand.

"You know you are going to get that a lot Amora! You're beautiful and it will cause some people to be extremely jealous of you" Pastor Damien told me calmly. Without responding I looked at my mother who seemed really irritated that Damien was even talking to me.

"That cut under your eye looks like it's infected. How would you like for me to take a look at it for you?" He asked.

"No Thank you!" I answered quickly "It's fine" I added.

"Yeah it's fine!" My mother said with so much attitude finally making her presence known. It was killing her that her attempt to break me was back firing. Everyone was still showering me with attention and calling me beautiful with so many black and blue marks on my face.

"Well Stephanie, I'm having a small get together at my home. I would love for you to come and for you to bring beautiful, I mean Amora" Damien said stumbling over his words.

"We will be there" My mother said while cutting her eyes at me then getting in the car.

"Okay well I will see you later beautiful and you too Stephanie." Damien said before walking away from the car and going back inside the church.

"You just couldn't shut up huh?" My mother yelled while looking at me through the rear view mirror.

"Mom I didn't even say anything to him." I replied confused.

"Yeah you did. I told you that you are not to talk to anyone, they ask about your face you tell them you got jumped and shut your dumb ass up!" She screamed.

"That's what I did!" I told her louder than I anticipated.

"Who do you think you're talking to Amora?" My mother yelled before slamming on the breaks and throwing a bottle of juice at me. It was the only thing she could get her hand on quick enough.

"Nobody mom" I said to her while ducking so the bottle wouldn't connect with my already swollen face.

"You must have lost your mind raising your voice at me Amora! Try it again!" She threatened. Deciding my best bet was to just remain quiet; I turned my head and looked out of the window the remainder of the ride home. My mother continued cursing and swearing at me, but I eventually tuned her out. I was tired of hearing the same ole name calling, same ole threats, same ole beatings. I couldn't understand what my mother wanted from me. She clearly didn't want me but wouldn't let me leave.

"Take your ass in the house and go straight to that room. I don't want to hear a peep out of you until I'm ready to go". She told me as she parked in front of our house. Quickly getting out of the car and running up the front steps, I rushed to get the key in the door before my mother had a chance to come up behind me and decide she wanted to crack me in my head again. After finally getting the door unlocked I went straight to my room. Pulling my laptop from underneath my mattress, I logged onto Facebook to see what my school friends had been up to since I haven't been able to go to school. After scrolling through my news feed I noticed that I had a few inbox messages from my school crush.

Instant messages:

Amina Dayton: why weren't you in school today?

Amina Dayton: day 2 where have you been?

Amina Dayton:????

```
Amora Smith: I've been sick.

Amina Dayton: what's wrong with you?

Amora Smith: I have a stomach virus

Amina Dayton: When you coming back to school?

Amora Smith: sometime next week

Amina Dayton: okay see you then

Amora Smith: okay :)
```

All I could do was blush! Nobody knew that I liked girls, I don't even think I understood what I was feeling I just knew I liked Amina and she definitely liked me too. Amina and I were in the same class and every day we would eat lunch together then talk all day long in and out of class.

"Amora unlock this door you don't pay no damn bills in this house!" My mother screamed while banging on the door and twisting the knob.

"Okay here I come" I yelled before quietly closing my laptop and putting it back underneath my mattress. I had to hide the laptop my school gave me because I didn't want my mother to take it from me. She had already took my cell phone and the TV out of my room so I had no type of entertainment. I was not about to let her find out about my laptop so she could take that too. Jumping off my bed and running to unlock my room door, I snatched the door open. "Yes?" I asked.

"Don't yes me! What are you in here doing?" My mother said as she pushed me out of the way and began to look around my room.

"Nothing" I answered quickly. "I was just lying down" I stuttered. My mother was so unpredictable in my eyes and I honestly feared her.

"Mmhmm" She replied. "Well come on so I can wash your hair then we can leave" She told me.

"Wash my hair why?" I asked with confusion.

"Because I said so" She yelled.

"I just washed my hair this morning though mom" I replied.

"Don't make me tell you again Amora. Come on!" She screamed while walking out of the room. I was so confused as to what was going on because there was no telling what my mother had up her sleeve. I slowly followed my mother down the steps and into the kitchen. She had the shampoo, conditioner and combs all set up on the towel with the water running. "Come on!" She told me calmly. Hesitantly I walked over to the sink and bent down so that my head was inside of the sink and directly underneath the faucet. "At what point are you going to start listening to me Amora?" She asked me.

"Huh? I do listen to you mom." I replied while trying to sit up.

"No you don't!" She said while forcing my head back down and putting the sink stopper in to allow the water to build up in the sink. Afraid of what my mother was about to do I began to panic.

"Mom I do listen to you!" I tried to reason while attempting to sit up again.

"When I tell you not to open your mouth to talk to people, that's exactly what I mean! Got people looking at me sideways and shit!" She screamed while wrapping her hand tightly around my hair then forcing my head down underneath the water. I struggled trying to get out of my mother's grip all while still holding my breath.

"I'm so sick of you after all I do to you; you're still here just die already!" She screamed at me in rage why still holding my head under the water. "Every time I turn around it always Amora this, Amora that, Amora is so beautiful, where is Amora, why is Amora sad, why is Amora crying, why are you so mean to Amora, I'm sick of hearing that shit." She continued to yell while yanking my head from under the water. Grasping for air and coughing vigorously I tried to run away from her forgetting that she had a fist full of my hair.

"Mom please stop! Let me go!" I cried.

"No! I wish you die already!" She screamed while forcing my head back down in the sink. I began to kick and use all of the strength I had left to push my mother back so that I would be able to lift my head from under the water. That only made her push me down harder so I stopped fighting back. I guess that's all she wanted because she immediately yanked my head from underneath the water then pushed me away from her. Unable to see or catch my balance I hit the wall then fell to the floor. Coughing up water and gasping for air I was relieved I could finally breathe and I was scared as hell so I jumped up and ran as fast as I could away from her and up to my room. Once I made to my room I cried so hard, I couldn't believe my mother tried to kill me. It hurt me to my core to hear her say that she wished I would just die. I really didn't understand what I could have done that was so bad for my own mother to feel this way about me.

"Get up and get dressed NOW! And be in the car in five minutes Amora"! My mother yelled from the bottom of the stairs. Not bothering to respond, I got out of bed and walked into the bathroom to attempt to fix my hair. Looking at myself in the mirror I stared at the damaged girl looking back at me. I was broken with no one to help me, I would often wonder why older people always said "take all your problems to the Lord and he will make a way," Yet here I was suffering knowing God can see and hear everything happening to me but did absolutely nothing to deliver me.

"Let's go Amora! Right Now!" My mother demanded.

"Okay here I come!" I replied while walking back into my room, throwing on a pair of jeans and white t-shirt and then slipping on a pair of sandals then running down the steps.

"I told you five minutes!" My mother scolded as soon as I got in the car.

"I went as fast as I could mom!" I told her while putting on seatbelt on.

"Next time go faster!" She demanded before turning the radio up to indicate she didn't want to hear nothing else out of me. Leaning my head back on the headrest I closed my eyes and reflected on why my life had to be so hard at such a young age. For the life of me, I couldn't figure out what my mother's problem was with me and why she treated me so badly. I felt like I was a burden on her but yet she never allowed me to go anywhere or leave for that matter.

It took us an hour and 45 minutes to arrive at Pastor Damien's house; he lived in Red Bank New Jersey. Driving into his housing community it reminded me of the neighborhood we used to live in before my parents divorced. The neighborhood we were forced to move into I was forced to become accustomed to dirty blocks, guys hanging on every corner, small section 8 homes and drug addicts walking up and down the street begging. As we pulled up to Pastor Damien's house my mother turned the music down and looked at me through her rear view mirror.

"The same thing applies Amora! Do not I repeat do not talk to anyone! They ask you what happened to you tell them what I told you and that's it! Don't hold any conversations with anyone if I'm not around and if Joseline is here stay away from her. Other than that find a corner somewhere and sit down until it's time to go! Do I make myself clear?" My mother said to me.

"Yes"! I replied then climbed out the car. Walking up to the house we could hear that the cookout was in full swing.

The smell of food and smoke from the grill filled the air. Music was blasting through the speakers and people were sitting around the yard dancing, talking and eating.

"Stephanie glad to see you made it!" Damien said as he walked over and hugged her. "Hello again beautiful!" He said as he reached over to hug me causing me to quickly move away from him before he could touch me.

"Hi" I greeted back. "Umm can you tell me where the bathroom is?" I asked him.

"Go straight through the front door all the way down the hall first door on your left!" He instructed and turned his attention back to my mother. Excusing myself and following the directions Damien gave me to the bathroom, I walked in and closed the door. Flopping down on the toilet, I ran my hands down my face. Not only did I not want to be around my mother, I damn sure didn't want to be anywhere near Damien and his extremely touchy feely self. Getting up and splashing water on my face, I prepared myself for an eventful evening that I was sure going to turn bad. Walking out of the bathroom fixing my shirt I began to walk down the hall until I felt the presence of someone behind me.

"You know it's rude to pull back when someone is trying to hug you." Damien said as stood behind me with his hands in his pockets.

"I didn't want a hug at the moment Pastor Damien and besides I really had to use the bathroom." I told him.

"That's interesting because I didn't hear the toilet flush so what were you really doing in there?" Damien asked as he walked closer to me.

"Umm I was just getting myself together." I stuttered backing away from him.

"You seem scared beautiful! Do I scare you?" Damien asked invading my personal space.

"No. Um yes! I mean I don't know." I replied bumping into the wall behind me.

"I'm not going to hurt you beautiful. I promise." Damien spoke as he began to my face.

"Ummm I need to go find my mom." I stuttered trying to walk around him.

"In due time beautiful! In due time I'll show you and I promise to be gentle." Damien said removing his hand from my face.

"Mmmhm" My mother said clearing her throat. "Amora what are you doing?" She asked me.

"I was umm using the bathroom and Pastor Damien stopped me on my way out." I told her.

"You're free to go beautiful." Damien said moving out of my way.

"Amora go do what I told you to do until I'm ready to go". My mother demanded.

"Okay!" I replied and hurried out of her sight.

"What was that about?" I heard my mother ask Damien as I walked off.

"You're jealous?" He asked ignoring her question.

"You're my man so why are you in her face?" My mother replied causing me to peek from around the corner I was hiding behind.

"I'm not only your man remember there is a list of others who were here before you don't ever forget that Stephanie." Damien replied before kissing my mother's cheek and walking away. My mother was furious at this point. I'm sure she knew how Damien operated, anyone with eyes could see that he juggled multiple women I think that might have been the first time he threw it in her face. I guess my mother knew when to leave well enough alone because instead of going after him or responding the way I knew she could have, she walked in the opposite direction and left Damien alone. She made it her business to however keep her eye on me through the remainder of our time there.

Present

"So you mean to tell me your mom was mad at you when her boyfriend was doing everything directly in her face?" Amora's student Sierra asked breaking Amora from the story she was telling.

"Yup, it was almost as if in her eyes I was the one doing wrong and he was the innocent one." Amora replied.

"How did that make you feel?" Sierra asked sympathetically.

"Sad... confused! I was confused because I didn't understand what I was doing wrong. She would tell me not to talk to people then they would come and talk to me. And if I ignored them I would get in trouble for being disrespectful, I just didn't understand what she wanted me to do." Amora expressed to Sierra before their conversation was interrupted by a knock at the door.

"Umm Amora it's after 5 so I am going to head on home, do you need me to do anything before I go?" Amora's assistant and best friend Sam said as she stuck her head inside of Amora's office.

"Dang is it?" Amora panicked as she checked her watch. "No I'm good Sam thank you and I'll call you when I get out of here" Amora told Sam as she turned her attention back to Sierra.

"Please don't tell me you have to end the story here, I need to hear more" Sierra spoke before Amora had a chance to.

"Unfortunately I do have to end it here but if you come see me tomorrow I promise I will continue" Amora reasoned with her.

"You promise?" Sierra asked her.

"You have my word, I'll see you tomorrow." Amora told her as she walked her towards the door.

"Okay Ms. Amora I'll see you tomorrow" Sierra said before hugging her and walking away. That small gesture was proof enough that Amora's made the right decision in forcing herself to open up in order to create a breakthrough for Sierra. Grabbing her phone, Amora dialed the only person she knew would be just as excited about today's events as she was.

"Hey my sweet baby" The caller spoke into the phone.

"Hey Gi, what's the matter? You don't sound like yourself" Amora replied.

"I'm good baby, a little tired but I'm good" Mrs. Gionna told her.

"You sure Gi, because you know I will fly to you in a heartbeat" Amora assured her.

"I know baby but you don't have to do that, God has me covered" Mrs. Gionna expressed.

"I know that's right! I was calling to tell you about the semi breakthrough I had today with one of my students" Amora began

"Is it that little smart mouth one? I would have been beat her little ass with my cane" Mrs. Gionna threatened causing Amora to laugh.

"Gi that's not nice." Amora told her laughing. "She is hurt and angry at the world because of who hurt her. She kind of reminds me of myself." Amora confessed.

"You were not disrespectful Amora! Hurt, abused, angry yes but never disrespectful! That little heffa needs her ass beat" Mrs. Gionna told her.

"Are you going to let me tell you what happened or are you going to keep telling me what she needs?" Amora asked.

"Oh hell no, Amora you're not too old for me to get you with my cane! Don't let this distance get to your head because just like you, I will hop my old ass on a plane so fast and help you remember who I am to you" Mrs. Gionna threatened.

"I'm sorry Gi, I just knew that would get your attention off of Sierra and her ways. I'm trying to tell you a story dang" Amora laughed and whined at the same time.

"Fine I'm listening! You're such a brat" Mrs. Gionna told her

"I know pray for me" Amora suggested "But anyway today at the center we had a workshop where I had a few female entrepreneurs come in and speak to the girls sharing some of their stories and what it took for them to get to where they are. One of the women brought up the fact that I helped her deal with somethings from her past and how lucky the girls were to have a mentor like myself to help guide them. Well after the workshop was over, Sierra and I had our weekly one on one session and I asked her how she felt about the workshop. She went on to say that the speakers weren't relatable because their circumstances growing up were a lot easier than hers and the other girls in the program. I proceeded to ask her why she didn't take it as motivation. So she broke down how hard life is for her to survive every day and until she can talk to someone who experienced "real life shit" as she puts it then my effort in helping her is basically pointless. It was in that moment Gi I knew my approach was wrong with the program because she was dead set on me having a perfect life growing up and having everything handed to me by my parents and rich boyfriend" Amora told her chuckling.

"That's what's wrong with these kids today they don't want to listen, they swear they are the first ones to go through stuff not even realizing that there are so many people out here that are actually going through the same thing or have been through it already" Mrs. Gionna interrupted.

"Exactly but I now know that's why I do what I do to show them that not only have I been through it but I've survived it and I learned from everything that has happened to me" Amora replied.

"I know that's right baby" Mrs. Gionna said with admiration. "So you told her your story?" She asked.

"Yes well I told her part of it, time got away from us and I had to close for the day but what got me was the fact that she was actually listening and wanted to know how I felt when certain things happened to me and get this Gi" Amora said to her.

"What's that babygirl?" Mrs. Gionna inquired.

"She didn't want me to stop telling the story she was so in tuned with it that she made me promise to finish telling her tomorrow" Amora told her.

"I thought you only saw her once a week" Mrs. Gionna asked.

"I do but I guess she felt so connected to my story that she wants to see me again tomorrow so that I can finish" Amora said.

"That is amazing! Amora let me ask you something" Mrs. Gionna said to her.

"What's that?" Amora asked.

"If you were able to create a breakthrough for one of the toughest girls in your program, imagine what you can do for girls around the world by just simply telling your story" Mrs. Gionna told her.

"Honestly Gi, I think I am ready" Amora replied.

"I'm so proud of you Amora! I want you to promise me something" Mrs. Gionna told her.

"Thank you Gi I don't think I could have made it this far without you" Amora confessed.

"You would have because it was already written, God brought me into your life because he knew I would be able to help guide you to your purpose" Mrs. Gionna told her.

"Since when did you become so spiritual?" Amora asked.

"Since you send me those damn sermons and scriptures every morning" Mrs. Gionna laughed causing her to cough uncontrollably.

"Gi you okay?" Amora asked concerned.

"Yes stop worrying about me, I will be fine! Now I want you to promise me something" Mrs. Gionna told her.

"Anything" Amora assured her.

"Promise me that every single thing you told me you were going to do to be the change you want to see around you. Promise me that you will do it! I don't care what attack the enemy sends your way, you fight through it and claim that victory that is yours! Do you hear me Amora?" Mrs. Gionna told her.

"Yes Gi and I will! I promise" Amora told her. "When I'm feeling weak I'll just come to you, your hugs and presence always make me feel like I can get through anything" Amora added.

"Awe baby I love that you feel that way but before me the strength you think I give you comes from one source and that's God! Trust in him before anything else, you taught me that" Mrs. Gionna told her.

"You're right Gi, I'm going to let you go! I have some notes and planning to do but I will see you this weekend for your birthday! I can't wait" Amora told her excited.

"Pray I can hold on until then" Mrs. Gionna replied.

"What you mean?" Amora asked concerned.

"Oh nothing chile I just mean I miss you so much I can hardly wait until this weekend!" Mrs. Gionna lied afraid to tell Amora what was really going on.

"I love you Gi and I'll see you in a couple days." Amora told her.

"I love you more baby girl!" Mrs. Gionna replied before hanging up the phone. Amora sat back in deep thought, digesting all of today's events then dropped to her knees for prayer.

"Father God I come to you right now asking for direction, God I know not what you're doing but I trust you! You've brought me out of and through so much that it's impossible for you to leave me now. Father guide me and give me strength, God give me peace and patience and allow me to seek you first in everything and depend solely on you! Father I only want your will and I believe you are doing something special with this program for these girl. God continue to give me wisdom and knowledge to help these girls seek you the same way Gi taught me to. Father bless Gi give her strength and continue to allow her to guide me to you. God continue to make me effective and bless me in ways that I am able to be a blessing to others and you get the glory and praise. Satan I bind the attack you're gearing up for against me and God I declare victory! In Jesus name Amen"

The next day Amora was seated at her desk awaiting Sierra's arrival when her thoughts were interrupted by one of her students who wasn't quite happy with her at the moment.

"Ms. Amora, how come you never got personal with us? We've never gave you as much attitude as Sierra did and you sitting up here telling her stories and what not. We want to hear about your childhood too" Amora's student Monae said as she barged through the door with her arms folded and four other girls standing behind her.

"I'm sorry Ms. Amora I couldn't keep it to myself how much alike you are to us. Like every last one of us stick together not because we enjoying clicking up but because we all understand what each other is going through because it has happened to every last one of us. So to see how you are now compared to what you've been through to get to where you are its causing me to look at you completely different and you didn't even tell me everything yet" Sierra told her as she made her way inside of Amora's office and made herself comfortable.

"Umm to answer your question Monae I didn't get to tell you all my story because you as well as the other girls were responsive to the advice I was already giving. I had to get personal to get through to Sierra but if Sierra doesn't mind you can join us as I continue telling her my story" Amora replied causing Monae to look in Sierra's direction.

"I don't mind, I just want to hear what happened next! Don't come in here asking a bunch of question either just sit and listen" Sierra told her friends as they all piled inside of her office.

"Be nice Sierra!" Amora told her shaking her head.

"We are not paying her any mind Ms. Amora, you can start" Monae replied.

"I'm going to assume that Sierra already told you girls the portion of the story I told her yesterday" Amora said to them.

"Yes" They replied in unison.

"Okay so about three weeks after the BBQ at Pastor Damien's house I was finally able to go back to school because all of my bruises weren't noticeable anymore" Amora began….

Past

"Amora I'm finished getting dressed! Are you getting up soon we don't want to miss the bus?" Sionni asked me.

"Yeah Sionni I'm getting up now! Go make you a bowl of cereal while I get myself together!" I told her before climbing out of bed. Grabbing my towel and shower cap, I walked into the bathroom being sure to close and locked the door behind me. I made a habit of doing that because I never knew who my mom brought home with her. After hanging my towel on the back of the door, I turned the water on and turned my attention to my reflection in the mirror. Running my hands through my now shoulder length hair I thought back to the night when my mother chopped my hair off.

"You're never going to learn are you Amora?" My mother asked me as she stood in the doorway of my room smoking a cigarette.

"What did I do now mom?" I asked with frustration evident in my voice.

"I told your ugly ass before we even got to Damien's house to go in there not talk to anyone find you a corner and sit down until I was ready to go! And what did you do? Go sneak off and be all in Damien's face." She yelled and accused me.

"I wasn't in his face! That man was in my face he followed me in that house when I said I had to use the bathroom. He stood outside that door and waiting for me to come out! He invaded my personal space touching my face and hair when I asked him to leave me alone and let me come find you! How did I do anything wrong?" I replied with my voice slightly raised. I couldn't believe she was trying to blame everything on me.

Leaping at across the room, my mother pulled me from my bed by my hair. "Bitch I told you to watch how you talk to me!" She said through clinched teeth.

"Mom I was just trying to explain to you that I didn't do anything! It was him! It was Damien." I screamed while trying to pry my mother's hand off of my hair.

"No it was you!" She screamed at me while dragging me down the steps. "No matter what I do or say motherfuckers just love telling me how beautiful you are. That nigga completely forgets about me when you come around!" She

rambled on while rummaging through the kitchen drawer looking for something in particular.

"Mom! Why are you doing this to me?" I asked between cries "I haven't done anything to you! I love you and you treat me like I'm nothing!" I continued to cry hoping she would let me know what I did wrong.

"Because I can't stand you, I can't stand to look at you, I can't stand to be in your presence and I can't fucking stand all the attention you get! What about me? Huh? Everybody just forgets about me when you're around." My mother vented while pulling out a pair of scissors and forcing me in between her legs to prevent me from getting away.

"Wait Mom No! what are you doing?" I asked frantically "I won't talk to anyone anymore! I won't be pretty anymore just please don't hurt me!" I cried.

"Fuck you!" She replied before cutting a huge chunk of my long and beautiful hair off and shoving it in my mouth. You want to be beautiful bitch? Let's see how pretty they think you are when I'm finished with you". She added while pushing me to the floor and stepping over me.

I loved my hair, I loved how curly and silky it was, the length made it that much better so when my mother cut a huge chunk of it off it forced me to have to cut the rest so that it would all be even. Looking in the mirror at the broken image of myself, I wondered how much more I could actually take. I felt like giving up, I did not want to endure the physical and emotional pain anymore. I honestly felt myself wanting to die, it didn't matter to anyone what my everyday life struggle was so I felt it wouldn't matter if I was gone or not. After showering and brushing my teeth, I rushed to get ready for school. I was somewhat excited to finally be leaving the house even though I hated being at school just as much as I hated being home. Wrapping my towel around my body, I opened the bathroom door and bumped into the last person I wanted to see.

"Good morning, beautiful how are you this morning?" Damien asked as he stood before me in nothing but his boxers.

"Fine!" I told him before walking around him and running into my room and locking the door behind me. With my back against the door I couldn't help but think that Damien was going to be a real problem, he just wasn't letting up! Walking over to the dresser I shared with Sionni, I began to search for something to wear to school. Not having much to choose from I decided to just throw on a pair of high wasted jean shorts with a white crop top and some sandals. Not liking how my curls fell now considering that my hair was no longer as long as it was. I decided to braid my hair in two French braids once I was finished I grabbed my book bag and met Sionni downstairs.

"You ready Sionni?" I asked as I reached the bottom step.

"Yeah I've been ready Amora you're the one that was taking all long." Sionni replied as she got up to turn off the TV.

"I'm ready now so grab your book bag and come on!" I told her and walked out the door.

"You look pretty today sister!" Sionni complimented me smiling.

"Thank you!" I told her with a smile on my face.

"What made you cut your hair though Amora?" She asked. "It was so long and pretty." She added.

"I don't know Si, just trying something different I guess" I lied. There was no way I could tell her what had really happened. Sionni already felt bad for me so telling her everything that has happened would hurt her even more than it hurt me to endure.

"Oh okay. Well I like it!" Sionni beamed.

"*I'm glad somebody likes it*!" I mumbled. "Come on Si run there go the bus!" I yelled while running to catch the bus.

"Well if it isn't beauty one and two. I haven't seen you girls on this bus in a couple weeks." Our bus driver Ms. Mary said.

"Good morning Ms. Mary!" We both replied in unison.

"Morning Ladies! Hurry up and take your seats so we can go!" Doing as we were told, both Sionni and I sat in our assigned seats before speaking to our friends that were already seated on the bus.

"Amora girl where have you been?" My best friend Sam asked me.

"Home sick with a stomach virus! I tried to hit you up on Facebook but you didn't reply." I told her.

"I haven't been on Facebook, but I texted and called you a thousand times and you never replied to me!" Sam said.

"I don't have my phone! My mom took it a couple weeks ago and won't give it back to me so the only way I can reach out is through Facebook because she doesn't know I have the laptop the school gave us." I told her.

"Well what you do that she took your phone?" Sam asked.

"Nothing bestie you know how she is!" I replied nonchalantly.

"Okay everyone make sure you have all of your belongings and I'll see you at 3pm!" Ms. Mary announced as she pulled the bus up to our school. Grabbing my book bag and checking to make sure Sionni was behind me, I got off the bus and walked through the school yard. Walking through the yard I stopped and turned around to face my sister.

"Okay Sionni I'll see you later." I told her before hugging her and walking away.

"You know Amina been asking about you best friend? What's going on with yall?" Sam smirked.

"Nothing going on and yeah I know she hit me on Facebook." I told her.

"You like her don't you?" Sam asked.

"You're really nosey you know that?" I told her.

"You're my best friend so your business is my business!" Sam said before putting her arm around my shoulder as the two of us entered the classroom and took our seats.

"About time you decided to grace us with your presence!" Amina said as she sat in the seat next to me.

"I told you I was sick!" I replied smiling. She used to make me blush so hard, I'm talking about cheeks red as hell.

"Yeah but you told me that three weeks ago. Glad you're feeling better though! Hey wassup Sam!" Amina spoke.

"Hey Amina girl!" Sam spoke back.

"Alright guys take out your projects and get ready to present. Amora I know you're behind, come see me after school and I will give you all of your work for you to make up!" Mrs. Greene told me.

"Okay I will!" I replied.

"Samantha you're up first!" Mrs. Greene announced interrupting a side conversation Sam was having with her boyfriend at the time.

"Dang, Mrs. Greene why you always picking on me?" Sam asked.

"Because you like to run your mouth so much now is the perfect time to do so now get your butt up here!" Mrs. Greene ordered causing the entire class to erupt in laughter. The remainder of class I watched as several of my classmates got up to present their projects and all I could think about was how happy I was to have been absent because I hated presenting in front of the class. I didn't like a lot of attention.

"Okay the remainder of you guys will present after lunch!" Mrs. Greene announced before dismissing us for lunch.

"Amora you're sitting with me right?" Amina asked walking up behind me.

"Yeah. Well Sam and I are!" I told her.

"No ya'll go head Ima go sit with the boys. You know I have to watch Bruce flirting self!" Sam responded.

"Okay crazy I'll see you after lunch then." I laughed and told her before walking off with Amina.

"You still don't have your phone?" Amina asked while we stood in line to get our food.

"No she will not give it back to me" I told her. "The crazy thing is; I didn't even do anything for her to take my phone. My mom is just crazy" I added shaking head.

"She needs to give it back because I hate having to log onto Facebook just to talk to you every day" Amina complained.

"Well if you really want to talk to me then that's what you're going to have to do for the time being until she decides to give me my phone back" I told her with attitude.

"Only because it's you" Amina said while smirking at me.

"Whatever girl" I replied blushing.

"What do you want to eat?" Amina asked me.

"Chicken Caesar salad with extra dressing and a fruit salad" I told her before walking off to go find us a table.

"I got you a water to drink" Amina said minutes later as she sat down with our food.

"That's all I ever drink so thanks!" I replied and popped a grape in my mouth.

"Welcome! So you gone be my girlfriend or what?" Amina asked abruptly. "I've been crushing on you since I started going here and being as though you have yet to say you're aren't into girls. I'm just going to assume that you are" Amina said to me.

"I like girls and I like you too but you flirt too much. I would punch you in the face if I was your girlfriend the way you be out here acting." I said causing her to smirk at me.

Present

"Wait Ms. Amora you're a carpet muncher?" Monae asked in disbelief causing Amora to laugh.

"A what?" Amora asked her.

"A carpet muncher! You know one of those girls that be munching on others girls downstairs parts." Monae said trying explain what she meant as polite as possible.

"If you're asking if I like women, then yes Monae I enjoy women" Amora told her.

"Ain't nothing wrong with it, now will you shut your mouth and let her finish" Sierra interjected.

"My bad" Monae replied.

"Now as I was saying…" Amora continued.

Past

"Well I don't have a girlfriend so I can do what I want. I want you to be my girlfriend though!" Amina said matter factly.

"I've never had a girlfriend, well nobody knows that I like girl's actually so we can't really broadcast it right now if I decide to be your girlfriend" I told her honestly.

"That's cool as long as I get to call you my girlfriend I don't care who knows!" Amina said to me smiling. The remainder of the day flew by and before I knew it, it was time for me to go back to the hell whole I called home.

"Did you behave today Sionni?" I asked as we walked home from the bus stop.

"Yes, well I got in trouble for telling Shannon to shut her pot lickers so I didn't get to play at recess." Sionni told me then shrugged her shoulders.

"You told her to do what? Why would you say that?" I asked laughing.

"Because she was saying mean things about you and I got mad I wanted to punch on her but I knew I would really get in trouble so I just said shut your pot lickers and she got upset because everybody started laughing" Sionni replied.

"Sionni there is always going to be people that will say and do mean things but you don't have to respond to them! And I don't want you getting into trouble trying to defend me to anyone I'm okay. Besides Shannon is younger than I am who cares what she says about me!" I explained to her.

"You're my sister nobody can say mean stuff about you, if she says it again I'm just going to take the punishment because I'm going to pop her right in the lips" Sionni told me in a very serious tone.

"Something is wrong with you little girl!" I laughed as we walked in the house.

"Hey mom" I spoke soon as soon as I walked the house.

"Si baby, How was school?" My mother asked Sionni ignoring me.

"It was good mommy!" Sionni replied hugging her.

"I got a surprise for you baby girl. Go change your clothes so I can show you." My mother told her.

"Can I go too?" I asked hoping she would say yes.

"Absolutely not, take your ass up in that room and don't come out!" My mother ordered.

"But.." I begin but decided to just do as I was told.

 "Sorry Amora" Sionni said as she walked in the room and began changing her clothes.

"Stop saying that Sionni, you have nothing to be sorry for" I told her.

"I know but it makes me sad when you're sad and I know you're sad so don't say you're not sad!" Sionni replied.

"I'll be okay Si, just go enjoy your surprise!" I told her before rolling over and deciding to just take a nap. I laid in the same spot until I heard the front door close indicating that my mother and sister had finally left and I was home alone. After making sure the coast was clear I reached under my mattress grabbed my laptop and logged onto Facebook. Before checking my notifications I decided to first update my status.

Status Update: Home alone on a Friday

Instant messages:

Samantha Bridges: Bestie ask your mom if you can come

over for the weekend! My mom said I can have a sleep over.

Amora Smith: She not going to let me bestie, so I'm not even going to bother.

Samantha Bridges: Still ask her bestie, want me to get my mom to call her?

Amora Smith: ABSOLUTELY NOT!! Just forget it bestie I'll

see you at school Monday

Samantha Bridges: Okay ® see you

Status Update: Wish things were different ☺

Instant messages:

Amina Dayton: Hey bae wyd?

Amora Smith: nothing bored in house by myself. Wyd?

Amina Dayton: at my cousin house. I miss u

Amora Smith: I miss u too

Amina Dayton: I know you said you didn't want to broadcast our relationship right now but can we at least update our relationship status on here?

Amora Smith: No Amina dang, just relax

I zoned out for a second thinking how crazy my mom would react if she found out that I was gay. I didn't have to think about it much longer because Amina decided she was ready for the world to know at that very moment.

Amina Dayton updated her relationship status from single to in a relationship with Amora Smith

Instant messages:

Amora Smith: Now would you go and do that? I told you I didn't want anyone to know right now you're going to get me in so much Amina dang.

Amina Dayton: uploaded a picture

I couldn't believe my eyes, I asked Amina to respect my wishes and not broadcast our newly relationship until I was ready. She completely disregarded my wishes and did what she wanted because she felt like people needed to know that me and her were a couple. To top it off Amina decided to upload a picture we took in the bathroom at school kissing and hugging and I could have fainted.

```
Instant messages:

Amina Dayton: I'm sorry bae

Amora Smith: Sorry?? Really Amina? That was way too
much

Amina Dayton: don't be mad bae it's already done I
won't do anything else I promise.
```

At this point I didn't have anything else to say to Amina, I could have argued with her and told her off but the damage was already done and there was no undoing it. Ignoring Amina's last message I slammed my laptop closed and put it back under my mattress. I silently prayed that nobody would show my mother the picture I was tagged in. Scared and frustrated I decided to finally take a much needed nap.

"SPLASHHHH Get the fuck up!" My mother ordered throwing a bowl of water on me waking me out of my sleep.

"Mom what you do that for?" I asked wiping my face with the shirt I was wearing.

"You got something you want to tell me Amora?" She asked me.

"No. what are you talking about?" I asked stumbling over my words.

"Ima ask you one more time Amora. Do you have something to tell me?" She repeated.

"No mom! I don't" I replied.

"Oh you don't huh? Then what is this?" She screamed shoving her phone with a picture of me and Amina kissing in my face.

"Ummm mom I can explain!" I said with fear evident in my voice.

"Explain what? The fact that you're gay and broadcasting it on the internet? You want to explain that to me?" She asked before punching me in the face.

"I didn't post the picture mom"! I cried holding my bleeding nose.

"I don't care who posted the picture it's up there on the internet. You think I want to see that? You think I want people sending me picture of your dumb ass kissing girls? Huh?" She asked landing another blow to my face then dragging me out of the bed by my hair.

"Amora I'll kill you before I allow you to be walking around here liking girls, no daughter of mines will be gay." My mother continued to rant as she punched and kicked me continuously. Unable to defend myself, I curled up into a ball and took the punches and kicks as best as I could praying that it would end soon. The next day my mother decided to take things a little further and force an intervention between Pastor Damien and I.

"Amora come the hell on! Don't make me call you again!" My mother yelled from the bottom of the stairs. Throwing my hair into a messy bun and slipping on my sneakers I rushed out of my room and down the stairs. "I'm ready!" I told her out of breathe from rushing.

"Let's go!" She said before walking out of the door. Running to catch up with her, I got in the car and put my seatbelt on.

"Mom where are we going?" I asked her.

"To the church!" She answered. Wondering why I had to come with her, I sat back and kept my mouth shut. Fifteen minutes later we were pulling up to the church. After parking and grabbing her bag, my mother got out of the car and told me to follow her. We both entered the church and she lead the way straight to Pastor Damien's office.

KNOCK KNOCK!

"Come in!" Pastor Damien yelled.

"Hey!" My mother spoke.

"How are you?" Damien asked her. "Hello beautiful" He said to me.

"Hi" I replied taking a seat on the couch.

"So Stephanie what was so urgent that you needed to meet with me?" He asked.

"I just don't know what to do" My mother said as she began to fake cry. "I try so hard to provide a better life for my kids but this one here just gives me a hard time" She lied. I was speechless, I couldn't believe how my mother was performing in front of Pastor Damien. She was laying it on thick with fake tears and everything.

"What happened?" He asked.

"Yesterday I received several calls and texts about a picture that was posted on Facebook of Amora hugging and kissing a girl. Not only that but they have it posted on there that they are in a relationship" She told him as she forced fake tears to fall from her eyes.

"Is that true beautiful?" Damien asked turning his attention to me.

"Yes!" I replied with my head down.

"You do know that being gay is a sin right? A unforgivable sin in the eyes of God!" Damien explained.

"No I didn't know that!" I replied. "But I can't help what I like!" I told him.

"That's nothing but the devil beautiful, woman are supposed to like men and men only!" Damien emphasized. "Come here!" He demanded. Looking at my mother, I halfway expected her to speak up however all she did was sit in the corner nursing her fake tears. Hesitantly I got up from the couch I seated on and walked over to Pastor Damien's desk.

"Have a seat!" He told me patting his lap.

"No I'm okay!" I replied told him.

"You heard what he said!" My mother intervened. Pulling me on his lap, Damien began to caress the side of my face.

"You know beautiful you are way too pretty to lower your standards and settle for a girl. You can have any and every guy you want, you don't want to ruin your life by choosing to live in sin and be labeled as gay" He told me.

"I don't really care what people think or have to say about me! I can't help or change who I am!" I replied removing myself from his lap.

"You should care! Your decisions not only affect you they affect your family as well! Look how this is hurting your mother!" He replied pulling me back down on his lap and wrapping his arms around my waist.

"Pastor Damien can you please let me go! This is making me feel uncomfortable!" I told him. Removing his hands from my waist, he placed both hands on each side of my head forcing me to face him.

"You will not be gay! It's just something I will not allow" Damien spoke. Not really sure of how I should take his last statement, I removed his hands from my face and got off his lap.

"Is it okay if I go sit in the car?" I asked my mother.

"Go head!" My mother said handing me the car keys. I practically ran out of Damien's office and out of the church.

"Hey there beautiful liar" Mrs. Gionna spoke waving to me as I paced back and forth in front of the church.

"Hi Mrs. Gionna" I spoke back.

"What are you doing in that crazy church in the middle of a Saturday?" She asked.

"My mom had to meet with the Pastor." I told her walking across the street and standing in front of her house.

"How have you been?" She asked "I see your face cleared up." She added while looking me over.

"Amora come on!" My mother yelled from across the street.

"Don't you see her talking to me devil lady" Mrs. Gionna yelled at my mother.

"Lady if you don't get out of my face. Amora don't make me tell you again" My mother threatened.

"I have to go. Bye Mrs. Gionna!" I told her.

"Alright baby I'll see you soon" Mrs. Gionna said before giving my mother the finger then going inside of her house.

"Who was that?" My mother asked as soon I got in the car.

"Mrs. Gionna she lives in the house I was standing in front of" I told her.

"She nosey as hell stay away from her Amora" She ordered and turned the radio up. Later that night I sat in my room writing in my diary as Damien's words continuously repeated themselves over and over in my head.

Diary Entry #1

It's crazy how adults tell you that your actions are wrong but instead of explaining thoroughly why they are they wrong they try to beat the right into you! How can my mother cry and scream about me liking girls when I've seen her deal with one on a personal level? How can Pastor Damien tell me about sin when I see him sin everyday on and off the pulpit? Then the whole "I won't allow you to be gay comment scared me, the look in his eyes it was almost as if he wanted me to get that I will not be messing with girls under his watch! Made me wonder what he is willing to do to ensure that! God If you're listening please protect me from Damien please God! I'll deal with my mother's beating if you just keep me protected from him!

"Are you awake in there beautiful?" Damien asked as he broke me from my thoughts and pushed my room door open.

"I'm getting ready to go to sleep Pastor Damien. You need something?" I asked him.

"Yeah actually I do. You!" He said matter factly.

"What do you mean?" I asked confused.

"Did you think about what I said to you earlier?" He asked.

"No I can't change who I am and I don't plan to" I told him.

"I can change it!" He told me walking into my room.

"Damien, please get out of my room you're making me feel really uncomfortable." I told him as he stood at the foot of my bed with his hands in his pants. Sitting up on the bed and pulling the covers over her body I screamed out my mother's name. "MOM!" I yelled desperately.

"Aww look at you. What you think she's going to do? Stop me?" He taunted before walking closer to me and tugging on the sheet I had covering my body.

"Please leave me alone!" I began to cry. "I didn't do anything to you, please just get out Damien" I begged him.

"Don't cry baby girl" He said as he wiped the tears that drowned my face.

"You know, you are very beautiful Amora, too beautiful, it's mesmerizing. Often times I look at you and get lost in those pretty grey eyes. Then my eyes travel down to that fully built body you've been blessed with" He divulged as he caressed my cheek before pushing my hair out of my face.

"Damien you shouldn't be in here; this is not right I'm only 15! What could you possibly want with me?" I asked and sobbed loudly. "MOMMM!!! Please come in here" I screamed again.

"That's just it beautiful, I like them young and untouched" He said while licking his lips and ripping the covers completely off of her body. "Enough talking baby, let me make you feel good" He said before throwing his large framed body on top of mines.

"No Damien, please get off of me. STOP!! Please don't do this to me" I screamed and cried hysterically and began to kick and scream wildly. "MOM HELP ME PLEASE!!

68

"Yes baby, daddy loves this sweet tight pussy. You love daddy don't you Stephanie?" Damien asked while still thrusting in and out of me. The two of them were behaving like it was only them in the room.

"You know I love you daddy, I'll do anything for you" My mother replied before applying more pressure on the pillow she was holding over my face.

"Daddy's cumin baby! Uncover her face, I want to look in her eyes as I cum all up in this sweet piece of heaven" Damien demanded. My mother snatched the pillow off of my face and watched as Damien leaned down, bit my neck and emptied his seed inside of me.

"Until next time beautiful" Damien told me as he climbed off of me and grabbed his pants off of the floor. Relieved that the torture was finally over, I grabbed the sheet to cover my body and watched as the two of them walked out as if nothing happened. Before closing the door, Damien winked and blew a kiss at me. I rolled over and let out a gut wrenching cry. Unable to hold back anymore I cried until no more tears fell.

Present

"Sierra why are you crying?" Amora asked stopping her story. Shaking her head no, Sierra continued to cry before getting up and running out of the room. Amora turned and looked at the other students who also had tears rolling down their faces.

"Anybody want to tell me what they are feeling at this exact moment?" Amora asked the group of girls.

"I can only speak for myself, my tears are of relief. Ms. Amora I know we give you a hard time but it because we've been hurt by adults that claimed to have loved and care about us but turned around and hurt us in more ways than one. So to sit here and listen to you tell us you've survived the exact thing we are living through is inspiring because it makes me believe that I can get passed this shit, I mean stuff too" Monae expressed causing Amora to get up and embrace her.

"I want you girls to know that I would never hurt you, I honestly want the best for you for all of you. That's the purpose of this program and what I do so that I can help the next generation for girls be better. I promise you girls there are some good people in the world who want to see you win and I hope that I am proofing that to you girls" Amora told them making sure to hug each girl individually.

"Ms. Amora you the shit girl. You should probably go check on Sierra though, I know she could use a hug right now." Monae told Amora.

"Watch your mouth Monae and I will. You girls sit tight, I'll be back in a minute" Amora told them and made her way into the bathroom where she was sure Sierra had disappeared to.

"Sierra are you in here?" Amora asked as she pushed the bathroom door open.

"Ms. Amora how did you turn out to be such a good person after something so ugly happened to you? Like I want to kill him for what he did and your mother too! Like how can you not hate them?" Sierra bombarded with questions full of emotions as she wiped her face with tissue.

"Because forgiving someone is easier and more peaceful than to hate and hold a grudge towards them. I can't imagine what my life would be like if I carried that hurt all of these years. I forgave them a long time ago even without an apology not for them but for me!" Amora explained.

"I can't do it, I can't forgive him Ms. Amora I can't" Sierra cried shaking her head from side to side.

"Yes you can and I will help you but you have to be willing to acknowledge and talk about what's been done to you. It's the only way to get that burden off of you" Amora told her.

"How are you like this? You're not human I don't know of anyone as nice and humble as you with such an abusive past" Sierra told her.

"Well now you do know of one person and you are going to be the second because if it's the last thing I do I will push you passed this hurt so you're able to walk in your purpose" Amora replied.

"Purpose?" Sierra questioned.

"Girl where have you been during any of our workshops? You're purpose is basically what you were created to do here on earth. It's using your gifts and talents to make a difference in the world" Amora explained.

"How do I figure that out? I never really thought much about my future let alone find out what my purpose is. I didn't feel like anything good would come my way until yesterday" Sierra broke down.

"Yesterday?" Amora asked for clarity.

"When I realized that someone who had a horrible past like me turned out to be this amazing person I've been giving a hard time. Ms. Amora I don't want to be bitter, I don't want to fail, I don't want to hurt anymore" Sierra confessed.

"Unfortunately Sierra I cannot promise you that you won't experience failure, hurt and or pain because truthfully I still experience that today. However I can promise that through whatever you face from this moment forward I will be right by your side helping you through it!" Amora promised her.

"Everything?" Sierra asked for reassurance.

"Yes as long as you become open to letting go of what has hurt you and work on wanting better for yourself I am with you! But you have to stop fighting, you have to control that mouth of yours and you have to apply yourself and put your energy into finding and operating in your purpose" Amora explained to her.

"Can you show me how you found your purpose and was able to move past everything?" Sierra asked.

"Of course! Come on let's go back into my office so I can finish the story. The answer to all of questions will be answered by time I am finished" Amora told her as they left the bathroom and joined the other girls back in her office.

"You cool Si?" Monae asked as Sierra walked in and took her seat on the couch.

"Yeah I'm good!" Sierra told her and smiled.

"Good! Now Ms. Amora can you get back to this story because I need to know what happened next" Monae asked eager to hear the rest of Amora's life story.

"Okay so the next day, my mother woke me up bright and early for church as if the night before never happened" Amora told them picking up where she left off.

Past

"Amora get up and get ready for church!" My mother screamed from the hallway. Rolling over to look at the clock, I rolled my eyes when I saw it read 7:30 am. Not bothering to respond to my mother, I tossed the covers off of my body then got out of the bed. When I stood up I noticed a puddle of blood in the middle of my bed. Panicking, I immediately pulled my panties down and noticed that there was blood there as well. Not knowing what it was from because it wasn't time for my period I called out to my mother.

"MOMMMMM!! Can you come here please?" I frantically screamed.

"What do you want Amora?" She yelled back.

"Something is wrong please come here!" I cried.

"What could possibly be wrong with you Amora?" She asked standing in the doorway.

"I'm bleeding!" I cried "And I'm not on my period!" I told her.

"That's what happens when a man pop that cherry stupid! She chuckled and walked away. Replaying last night's incident, I pulled out my diary and began to release my feelings.

Diary Entry #2

Anger, hurt, shame, embarrassment, fear are all these emotions are surrounding me. I cannot even begin to explain what it feels like to basically be raped into being straight. Do they not know that this just makes me hate men that much more? I am a child, my innocence was taken from me, my purity was damaged. I don't know what I feel anymore; I don't know of anything worse that can happen to me. After this I really question if there really is a higher power, how could he allow this to happen to me? How could he not protect me? How am I able to protect myself from the ones that are supposed to love and protect me? They are the ones doing the harm to me, it hurts that I was born into the lives of such evil people. How could she lay there and hold a pillow over my face and allow him to do that to me? Is it because she found out I was gay? Or was that just the excuse they're using to do what he wanted to do to me anyway? As my tears fall while I write this I begin to feel numb because I wonder if things will ever get better. God I thought you would protect me!

"Amora get your ass out that room and get ready like I said!" My mother screamed bringing me from my thoughts. Wiping the tears from my face and hiding my diary, I grabbed my towel and went to do what I was told. I stayed in the shower for about 45 minutes attempting to scrub off the scent and feeling and of Damien touching, kissing and having his way with me. I scrubbed my body until I could no longer take the pain. I wished I could wash the memory away completely but I knew it would forever be embedded in my mind.

"You got fifteen minutes Amora!" My mother screamed from her room.

"Okay!" I replied then walked into my room and began to get dressed. Deciding on a pair of straight leg dark denim jeans and a t-shirt, I slipped on my sandals threw my hair in a sloppy bun on top of my head, grabbed my bag then walked down the stairs before my mother could call out to me again.

"Oh you call yourself listening today?" She said to me. I didn't bother to respond; I just couldn't win for lose with her. I did everything I was asked and it still wasn't enough, she found something wrong with everything I did. Not to mention I was still in pain from the previous night's events so I didn't want to chance her getting mad over my response and making the pain worse.

"Come on!" My mother said snapping me from my thoughts. She held the door open for me to walk out before her.

"Stop walking like that!" She told me. "The way you're walking is going to have people all in our business" She added.

"I can't help it! I'm in pain!" I replied.

"Well you better suck it up and do what I said!" She told me sternly while getting in the car and starting it up.

"If ya'll would have never did this to me we wouldn't have this problem!" I mumbled angrily as I climbed in the car.

"What did you just say?" She asked.

"Nothing! I didn't say anything." I replied sarcastically as she pulled off and headed to the church. Fifteen minutes later my mother was parking in her favorite parking spot, right in front of the church.

"Let's go Amora!" She ordered. I got out of the car and followed close behind her as we passed through the crowd of people that filled the church. Making our way to the seats that we normally sat in, we sat down and watched as the praise and worship team lead praise and worship.

"Hello there beautiful!" Sister Joseline whispered to me from behind.

"Hi!" I spoke back over my shoulder.

"Everyone stand as we welcome the man of God." The worship leader announced over the microphone as Pastor Damien made his way into the sanctuary and onto the pulpit. I was disgusted by the way everyone in the church was praising him not knowing what kind of man he really was. Looking and listening to Damien scream about how good God was and how he was only there to lead his people to heaven infuriated me so much. Here he was pretending to be this perfect man when in fact he was a sick rapist. Just the night before he raped me and today he was on a pulpit preaching the gospel of Christ. What a joke!

"Today the lord has put something on my heart to address" Pastor Damien began. "Our children need us, they are confused about what it means to be saved, what it means to sin! What is a forgiven sin and what isn't" He continued. "They are manipulated by the devil himself into confusing what God placed and what is Satan sent. What am I talking about you ask? I am talking about homosexuality" He paused and looked at me making my palms sweat. *Is this really happening right now*? I thought to myself.

"I received a call earlier this week from one of our church members, completely distraught because she found out her daughter was kissing and messing with girls. I sat and I met with both of them and informed the young girl that the temptation she was experiencing was the devil. God created men to be with women and vice versa. Homosexuality is an unforgiven sin and it is not to be tolerated on any level". He preached receiving a crowd roar of Amen's from all of the brain washed members of the church. "I sat and talked to this young lady and I'm hoping I got through to her matter fact I believe she is here this morning." He announced pretending to look into the crowd. "Amora? Are you in this service?" He spoke into the crowd. I felt as if I was going to pass out so I sat there frozen unable to move, I couldn't believe that this was happening to me. Not only was he telling my business, but he was chastising me knowing good and well he didn't talk to me. That man forced his penis inside of me as punishment.

"Amora get your ass up there!" My mother scolded through clenched teeth. Hesitantly I stood to my feet and joined Damien in front of the entire congregation.

"The young girl I was referring to is this beautiful young lady right here," Damien said pulling me into him. "I want everyone to keep this young girl in each and every one of your prayers. Pray that God wins this battle with her life and that she is strong enough to be delivered from the devil's temptation he has placed in her mind." He preached. Completely embarrassed but unable to shed a single tear from this humiliation, I stood there with a blank look on my face as I watched several members come in front of me and lay their hands on my head repeating. "In the name of Jesus I declare you are delivered". This lasted for 20 minutes before Damien declared it was enough and sent the remaining church members back to their seats.

"I hope I was of some assistance in helping you overcome this trying time in your life," Damien whispered to me before kissing my forehead and sending me back to my seat. Feeling myself become extremely hot and unable to breathe I began to hyperventilate so I grabbed my mother's arm.

"I can't breathe!" I told her gasping for air.

"Well go outside and catch your breath," She told me unconcerned. Removing myself from my seat, I rushed through the sanctuary and outside. Once I made it outside I grabbed my chest and began to try to breathe deeply.

"You're taking too short of breaths honey! Take a real deep breath and slowly exhale it," Mrs. Gionna coached as she walked over to me. She was sitting on her porch being nosey as usually when she saw me. Doing as I was told, I began to take long deep breaths.

"That's it! Pretty just like that! One more" Mrs.Gionna instructed.

"Thank you!" I told her once I was able to talk.

"No need to thank me chile, I saw that you needed help and I couldn't sit back and doing nothing. You called me nosey and look I just almost saved your life." Mrs. Gionna joked. "Where is that devil mother of yours while you out here fighting through panic attacks by yourself?" She asked.

"Inside the service," I told her with sadness evident in my voice.

"Did she know you were having a panic attack?" Mrs. Gionna asked me.

"Yes, she told me to come out here and catch my breath" I replied.

"That stinking heffa, I should go in there and slap her silly" Mrs. Gionna cursed.

"You are funny!" I told her laughing at what she said.

"If only you knew that I was serious little girl" Mrs. Gionna said to me. "Come on, ain't no use in going back in that devil's pit! I'll make you something to eat and we can chit chat" She offered.

"Okay!" I agreed without any hesitation.

"Why are you walking like that?" Mrs. Gionna asked with a raised eyebrow stopping me in my tracks.

"Like what?" I replied unable to think of a lie on the spot.

"Nothing come on!" Mrs. Gionna told me catching on to the hesitation in my voice. Walking across the street and into Mrs. Gionna house, I made myself comfortable on the couch while she walked into the kitchen.

"I have some leftover shrimp and chicken Alfredo from last night is that okay?" Mrs. Gionna asked.

"Yes I love pasta!" I told her excited that I was about eat my favorite food, I was just praying she could cook.

"Here you go suga." Mrs. Gionna said five minutes later handing me a plate of Alfredo with a side of broccoli and garlic bread.

"Thank you!" I said before digging in with no remorse.

"Slow down baby! That damn food isn't going anywhere!" Mrs. Gionna joked.

"Sorry" I said to her. "I haven't had a home cooked meal in I don't know how long it's only cereal, peanut butter and jelly or oodles and noodles for me on a daily basis so I appreciate this very much" I told her with a mouth full of food.

"No apologies needed!" Mrs. Gionna replied. "So that devil you call a mother don't cook for you?" She asked.

"She cooks when my sister is home sometimes but when she is away no she doesn't. And she tells me not to touch her stove, so I'm left to eat everything that doesn't involve being cooked on the stove." I told her.

"Well where is your sister and why aren't you with her?" She asked.

"She is with my aunt for the summer. I'm not allowed to go over there or anywhere for that matter. I can't tell you why because I don't know why." I told her quickly answering the question I knew was sure to follow.

"So you go from school to home and from home to that bulshit of a church?" Mrs. Gionna asked.

"Yup that's pretty much my life!" I said putting my fork down and sitting my plate on the table.

"Why is that, if you don't mind me asking?" Mrs. Gionna asked.

"I honestly don't know! Mrs. Gionna I'm not a bad child, I listen, I'm not sneaky, outside of hiding the fact that I like girls from my mother, but other than that I listen. I'm great in school, I have a good attitude but she just doesn't see it. It's like she has something against me. She finds any reason to hit or curse me out about." I told her.

"So what I saw her do a few weeks ago outside that church, is that something she does to you on a regular?" Mrs. Gionna asked.

"Yes, Mrs. Gionna" I replied and let the tears I was holding back fall. "I can't hold it in anymore. I'm beaten, cursed at, anything you can think of she does to me. I do absolutely nothing to deserve it but she just continues to treat me so bad. A few weeks ago she cut a chunk of my hair out because she was mad at her boyfriend so she took it out on me. A week before that, she stuffed my head in a sink full of water trying to drown me. Mrs. Gionna I am only fifteen this can't be what life is all about. If it is I want my life to end now!" I said with nothing but seriousness in my voice.

"I don't ever want to hear you say that Amora. There is going to be people all throughout life who are going to talk down to you, do mean things to you, some may even try to harm you but you know what? God prepared you early for it, so when it comes around again, which it will, you will have the strength and the armor to withstand anything that comes your way and fight it the hell off! I see the strength and fight in you but I also see the hurt in you. Use that hurt baby to keep fighting, there is light at the end of your tunnel. A bright light you just keep fighting to see exactly what I'm talking about." Mrs. Gionna told me as she rubbed my back. "It's okay to cry, shit my old ass cry sometimes but it's even better to not allow whatever is causing your tears to break you!" She told me.

 Later that night I tossed and turned in my sleep from the consistent nightmare that has been haunting me since the rape!

"I should kick your stupid ass down the steps, you're pregnant Amora?" My mother yelled as she stood in the

bathroom door watching me throw up for the third time this week.

"Grgggg" I couldn't even respond. "I don't know Grggg what's wrong Grggg with me" I said in between throwing up.

"You are pregnant stupid" She yelled. "I can't believe this. As much as I suck and fuck this nigga I am not pregnant yet but your dumb ass gets pregnant just from one fuck!" She cursed.

"If I'm pregnant it's because you and your sick boyfriend raped me! I was a virgin I've never allowed anyone in between my legs until that sick man came and forced himself on me and you helped him" I screamed at my mother.

"Who you think you're talking to?" She asked as she grabbed a fist full of my hair then forced my head in the toilet full of throw up.

"First thing Monday you're going to the abortion clinic and getting that damn baby sucked out of you" My mother said as she pulled my head out of the toilet. "There is no way in hell you will be walking around here carrying my man's baby and I can't even get pregnant by his ass" She added before kicking me in the stomach.

Jumping out of my sleep covered in nothing but sweat and tears, I immediately grabbed my stomach. I hoped and prayed God didn't hate me that much to curse me with a child that young and a child by Damien at that.

Present

"Ms. Amora I'm sorry to have to tell you this, but we are going to find your mom and beat her ass!" Monae spoke with anger as the other girls shook their heads in agreeance.

"What did I tell you about that mouth of yours Monae? And there will be no ass beating" Amora told them trying hard to contain her laugh.

"I'm sorry Ms. Amora but I'm with Monae on this one, your mom is out of pocket. How did she even produce someone like you? She is purely evil" Sierra spoke up.

"You just made a promise to me not even an hour ago and you're already trying to break that promise Sierra" Amora joked standing to her feet and placing her hand on her hip.

"I know but that shit ain't right" Sierra expressed shaking her head.

"First of all use your proper English and secondly I did not tell you about my past for you girls to defend it for me. I got through it! Everybody that has done me wrong has to deal with God. I don't have to get revenge on anyone. I'm not telling you this to upset you but I want you girls to learn from it, you understand what I'm saying? Understand that all the ugly that was done to me, built this beautiful person you girls admire" Amora explained to them.

"God needs to whoop your mother's ass then!" Monae replied and rolled her eyes.

"He definitely dealt with her and Damien as well" Amora told them.

"Really, How please tell me because he better had got them good" Sierra replied.

"You will see" Amora spoke before picking up where she left off.

Past...

It was the last day of school before summer vacation and I was excited but sad at the same time. I was happy the school year was coming to an end but was sad because outside of school, I had no other outlet from home, well except for Sundays when I go to visit Mrs. Gionna. Rushing to get ready for school, I was dressed in record time. After showering and getting dressed, I braided my hair in two braids which had become my signature style. I grabbed my bag and headed straight out the door and to the bus stop. Arriving at the bus stop the same time as the school bus I waited until the doors opened before I climbed on.

"Good morning pretty girl!" Mrs. Mary spoke as she opened the bus doors.

"Good morning Mrs. Mary" I spoke back and smiled.

"Amora I missed you!!" Sionni screamed as soon as she spotted me getting on the bus. It's been a couple weeks since we've last seen each other.

"Hey Si, I missed you too! I replied hugging her.

"You okay? I tried to call you the other day and mommy told me you were in trouble" Sionni said.

"Really" I asked. "I don't know why but you know how mommy is!" I told her taking a seat next to her.

"How is it over Aunt Sunny's house?" I asked her.

"It's so much fun, I seen daddy the other day, he took me for ice cream and I met his new wife." Sionni informed me.

"His wife? That's interesting." I said shaking my head. I often wondered how my father could put all this time in with these women and not even attempt to see what was going on with his daughters.

"Yes, and she's pretty Amora. She is nice too" Sionni said me.

"That's nice" I replied. "How have you been though Sionni? Have you talked to mommy a lot?" I asked her.

"Yeah she called me yesterday and told me she wanted to come take me on a girl's day because she missed me!" Sionni replied.

"That's nice" I replied salty.

"Okay kids yall know the drill. Have a great last day see yall munchkins at 3pm" Mrs. Mary announced and let all of us off the bus.

"Sionni, go ahead to class I will see you later" I told her. "Sam, come here really quick!" I called out to my best friend.

"Wassup bestie?" Sam asked walking over to me.

"We need to skip school today. I need to find out if I am pregnant or not. I keep having these nightmares and they are scaring me. Sam what am I going to with a baby? I can't even take care of myself! Man why is God punishing me?" I said in one breathe.

"Wait a minute! Pregnant, by who? I thought you and Amina was together? How in the heck did that happen? I do know that's not possible with a female so I know you're keeping something from me! Spill it bestie" Sam demanded.

"I will explain everything later Sam I promise but please just skip school with me today!" I begged.

"You know I got you!" Sam laughed and hugged me. We both walked in the opposite direction of our school and made our way to the Walgreens that was two blocks away.

"Hello welcome to Walgreens!" The sales clerk greeted.

"Hello!" We spoke back in unison.

"Let me know if I can be of any assistance to you ladies" The sales clerk said to us.

"As a matter of fact, you can" Sam spoke up. "We are looking for pregnancy tests. We need your cheapest one though lady" Sam informed her.

"Okay right this way ladies" The sales clerk laughed and led us down the aisles to the section where the pregnancy tests were. " Okay so we have a variety but since your friend here said you guys want the cheapest, here is the cheapest one we have and it's accurate so don't worry" She told us.

"We will take it!" Sam spoke before I could say anything.

"Sam dang let me have an opinion." I fussed.

"You're taking too long and we need to know like now!" Sam said to me. "Miss we will take that one can you ring us up please." She added.

"Sure you can follow me to my register!" The sales clerk told us.

"Do you have a Walgreens card?" She asked.

"No we don't need one, just need to pay for this thanks" Sam told her.

"Okay your total is $10.49." She said after scanning the test.

"Dang! I thought you said this was the cheapest one!" Sam frowned as she pulled the money out of her book bag. Handing the money to the clerk Sam turned to face me. "You lucky I love you bestie because I don't just be spending my moneys on anybody." She fussed.

"I love you too Sam!" I laughed.

"$.51 cent is your change, have a great day and good luck!" The sales clerk said to us as she handed Sam her change.

"Thank you!" Sam said taking her change and grabbing the bag. "Come on bestie" She said to me as we both walked out of the store. "Now where in the heck are we going to go for you to take this test and where are we going to do until school is over?" Sam asked.

"I don't know! You just had all the answers a few minutes ago don't stop now." I told her sarcastically.

"Shut up girl! You don't know anybody house we can go to until 3? Sam responded.

"Mmm no, wait yeah come on, I just hope her crazy self is home." I told her thinking of Mrs. Gionna. We caught the city bus to Mrs. Gionna house and thirty minutes later we were walking up the block she lived on.

"Bestie what's going on with you and Amina?" Sam asked.

"Girl nothing I broke up with her after she pulled that stunt on Facebook!" I replied.

"Dang for real? How you feel about that? I know you really liked her with your gay self!" Sam joked.

"I did but it was just too much, I didn't even tell you my mom almost caught her at my house the other day" I told her.

"You're lying!" Sam responded dramatically.

"Seriously, I told her I thought we should break up and she didn't want to so she asked me could she come see me to talk to me. First we were sitting outside then she asked if she could use the bathroom next think I know we ended up in my room kissing and fooling around until I heard my mom screaming my name. I almost died I pushed her in my closet so fast" I told her.

"So wait how did you sneak Amina out?" Sam asked.

"My mom only came home to change her clothes so when she screamed my name she was telling me to bring her overnight bag down stairs and some shoes out of her closet then she left" I replied.

"That's crazy! Wait Amora isn't that your mom car?" Sam asked and pointed as we walked up to Mrs. Gionna's house. Feeling my heart beat rapidly I hurried and turned my back in hopes that nobody seen me. Running up Mrs. Gionna's front steps, I rang the doorbell and knocked frantically.

"Who the hell is ringing my god damn bell like that?" Mrs. Gionna cursed and peeked through the window. "Amora what the hell. What's wrong? Wait why are you not in school?" She bombarded with questions.

"I'll tell you later can you let us in please?" I begged.

"Who the hell is "us"?" She asked not moving from the window.

"Omg! Mrs.Gionna come on! It's my best friend Sam" I told her pulling Sam in view of the window so she could see her. Unlocking the door and opening it Mrs. Gionna let us inside. "You're in now tell me why yalls asses are not in school and sitting in my damn living room?" Mrs. Gionna sassed with her hand on her hip and her cane in the other. Mrs. Gionna wasn't your average lady, she was crazy as hell. She was 4'11 medium built with beautiful smooth caramel skin, hazel slanted eyes and long silky jet black hair. She had a bad back which caused her to walk around with a cane all the time. A cane she didn't necessarily need because she hit people with it more than she used it to walk.

"Umm well see, Sam here has a problem we couldn't solve in school so we decided to just skip and being as though it's the last day we can't really get in trouble. You feel me?" I joked trying to hide the fact that I was lying.

"Hell no I don't feel you nor do I believe that nonsense you just fed me" Mrs. Gionna said as she walked passed both us and into the kitchen. Twenty minutes later, she filled each of our plates with French toast, cheese eggs and bacon. "Baby girl come help with these plates" She yelled out to me.

"Mmmmhmm it smells so good in here" I said as I grabbed my plate off the counter and walked back into the living room. "Sam you better go get your plate, my hands was full that's why I didn't grab it for you!" I told her.

"Bestie you have two hands though you always being smart" Sam said getting up and mugging me before running into the kitchen. "Thanks Mrs. Gionna" Sam said as she picked up her plate and came back into the living room and sat next to me.

"You have more bacon than me! Let me get a piece!" I told her trying to snatch the bacon off of her plate.

"Nope" Sam told me snatching her plate away. "Should have got my plate when you got yours and I would have shared" She teased.

"Oh whatever" I laughed digging back into my food.

"So which one of you young ladies would like to start first" Mrs. Gionna said as she sat across from us with her plate of food.

"Dang Mrs. Gionna can we at least eat first and get our thoughts together?" I joked trying to stall for time.

"Nope, sure can't! You can eat and talk just like your ass was just doing. And since you have so much to say Amora, let's hear it" Mrs. Gionna demanded. Sitting my plate on the table, I began to fidget with my hands. "Well umm I already told you Sam had a problem that we needed to solve and we didn't have anywhere else to go so we came here." I lied.

"Yeah you told me that, and I told you that it was a lie. I already told you I hate liars Amora, so tell me the truth! Since when do you have to lie to me?" Mrs. Gionna asked me.

Dropping my head, I took a deep breath and braced myself for Mrs. Gionna's reaction once I told her what was really going on. "Well Mrs. Gionna I've told you everything that was done to me except one thing" I began "A few weeks ago Pastor Damien who is my mother's boyfriend raped me because my mother told him I was gay" I confessed with tears streaming down my cheek.

"Omg bestie are you serious?" Sam asked attempting to put her arm around me. Putting my hand up to stop her, I shook my head no.

"No Sam I'm okay, I want to get this out. My girlfriend well ex-girlfriend put a picture of us hugging and kissing on Facebook, I asked her not to but she did it anyway. Someone sent the picture to my mom and she came home and beat me up. The next day she brought me to the church and cried in front of Pastor Damien about how she do all she can for me and I just give her such a hard time and a bunch of more lies. That night Damien came into my room and raped me with the help of my mother who held a pillow over my face to stop my screams" I said sniffling. "Then after he raped me he called me in front of the church and told the entire congregation that I was gay had all of them come and lay hands on me as if I was possessed or something" I continued. "Since the night I was raped I've been having nightmares about being pregnant so we skipped school today and brought a pregnancy test so that I can find out if I'm really pregnant or not" I confessed lifting my head up and looking at Mrs. Gionna who had a face full of tears.

Wiping her face with a napkin, Mrs. Gionna cleared her throat. "Mmhmm, Go ahead and take the test" She ordered. "Excuse me for a moment I need to get my thoughts together" She told us then left the room.

"Bestie I'm so sorry that happened to you" Sam cried and hugged me. "I mean I know your situation at home is bad but I didn't know it was like that. That is really sick of both of them. Do you want me to tell my mom? You know she will call the cops and have you out of there in a second" Sam asked reaching for her phone inside of her book bag.

"No Sam, please don't say anything! I don't want to make things any worse than they already are" I told her.

"You have to tell somebody Amora, something has to be done. It can happen again with you still being in the house" Sam replied worried for me

"Not yet Sam, I can't I don't really have family well I do but they won't help and I know your mom will help but I really don't want anyone to know" I said as I got up grabbed the pregnancy test and walked into the bathroom. Closing and locking the door behind me, I walked over to the sink and looked at myself in the mirror. *"Whatever this test reads, you're going to be okay. You have no choice but to be"* I said to my reflection. Taking the test out of the box and pulling my pants down, I peed on the stick being sure to follow the step by step instructions listed on the box. Ripping a piece of toilet tissue off of the roll and laying it on the sink, I laid the test on top of it and waited. That was the longest three minutes I've ever experienced. Picking the test up and seeing the single solid line, I breathed a sigh of relief then threw the test in the trashcan. Washing my hands, I opened the bathroom door and came face to face with two very anxious people.

"Well what did it say?" Sam asked as soon as I opened the bathroom door.

"I'm not pregnant!" I told them with a half smile.

"Thank you Jesus!" Mrs. Gionna shouted with her cane raised in the air.

"I'm so happy you're not pregnant bestie, you did not deserve that and that baby would have been a constant reminder of what happened to you." Sam told me sympathetically.

"Fast tail here got some sense." Mrs. Gionna joked in an attempt to lighten the mood.

"Mrs. Gionna you're crazy" I said before walking into Mrs. Gionna's open arms and laying my head on her chest letting out the tears desperately trying to fall.

"It's okay baby, let it out!" Mrs. Gionna told me and she held my head with one hand and rubbed my back with the other.

"I don't understand it, why me? Why do I have to go through all of this?" I cried.

"Baby everything you're going through is for a purpose so that later in life, not only will you have the strength to take on anything and fight through it, but also so that you can have a story to tell about what you've overcame" Mrs. Gionna said to me.

"It's just too much Mrs. Gionna, I try to be strong, I try not to allow it to break me but it hurts. I'm such a good person and I have big dreams but I'm slowly getting discouraged. Sometimes I even wonder if I will live long enough to see my dreams through. The hatred my mom has towards me and the frequent attacks makes me wonder if one day she is going to go all the way and just kill me" I cried harder. "Why does she hate me? Why won't she love me Mrs. Gionna? I just don't get it" I asked her.

"I know it hurts baby, I can only imagine how you're feeling but you have to be strong Amora, you cannot allow yourself to give up on life. I promise it will get better, pain does not last forever. God has something extremely great in stored for you so what you're going through now is only preparing you for the amazing person you have been called to be. Keep fighting baby you hear me!" Mrs. Gionna said forcing me to look at her.

"Yes, I hear you!" I replied shaking my head allowing more tears to fall.

"Amora if you don't understand anything else I need you to understand this. Your little stubborn, beautiful, sassy yet sweet, intelligent smart mouth butt made a huge impact on my life in such a short amount of time. If you feel like no one else loves you, I want you to always know that your Gi loves you and I will always be here. You understand me? I love you so much and I will never leave you okay?" Mrs. Gionna told me.

"You promise?" I asked her as I lifted my head and looked at her.

"I promise baby" She replied pulling me in for a much needed hug. "Now on a more serious note, that devil you call a mother, I'm going to get her! Mrs. Gionna threatened. "That ass is mines!" She added. "Amora take this cell phone and you make sure you call me the next time either one of them motherfuckers lay a finger on you! You hear me? Cause I'm coming to fuck shit up! You feel me?" She asked mimicking what I said to her earlier.

"Yeah I feel you Gi" I laughed.

"Mrs. Gionna, can you be my Gi too? That moment yall just had touched my heart" Sam said to her, holding her hand over her heart.

"No you little fast tail girl now, go on head and sit down somewhere" Mrs. Gionna said dismissing Sam.

"Dang Sam what that salt taste like?" I teased as we walked back in the living room and sat on the couch.

"That is one mean lady bestie, why does she like you so much" Sam asked salty

"Because I'm so lovable duh" I joked. "No but honestly I really don't know, we just clicked it's like she understands me like fully understand me. She can just feel when something is wrong with me before I even tell her. I think she's psychic or something," I stated seriously.

"I'm not no damn psychic girl" Mrs. Gionna said rejoining us in the living room.

"Dang Gi you're so nosey, how you hear that all the way in the other room? I wasn't even that loud," I laughed.

"I hear everything little girl, I keep telling you that. Now yall come on so I can get yall back over to that school cause yall not sitting around here getting on my nerves all day," Mrs. Gionna told us while looking for her car keys.

"Gi we can't go to school this late and on the last day, they are going to tell us to go back home. Why are you trying to kick us out?" I asked her.

"I have things to do little girl, despite what you may think I actually do stuff other than sitting in my window being nosey" Mrs. Gionna replied finally locating her keys.

"Well can we stay here until it's almost time for school to be out?" I asked. "It's already 12:30 we have to leave at 2 to make sure we make it back in time to catch the school bus home".

"Amora you live around the corner, why on earth would you go all the way back to school just to come back?" Mrs. Gionna asked me.

"Um Gi, if I go home from here I will get home too early and my mom will wonder how I got there so fast" I replied.

"Right, I knew that smart ass!" Mrs. Gionna replied. "Look whatever, just don't mess up my house and little fast tail girl you make sure you don't take anything that doesn't belong to you. I don't know you like that and I'm not saying you're a thief, I'm just saying I don't know you like

that so I don't go exploring and what not" Mrs. Gionna
said.

"I don't steal, so you have nothing to worry about" Sam
told her.

"Okay, well let me get going. Amora remember what I
said, use that phone and call me if you need me cause I will
come blazing for my baby. You feel me?" Mrs. Gionna told
me.

"Gi please do not say that anymore" I laughed. "But I will I
promise!" I assured her.

"Make sure you lock up when y'all leave and I'll see you
Sunday" Mrs. Gionna told me kissing my cheek then
hugging me before walking out the door.

Present

Knock Knock!

"I don't mean to interrupt but. Woah you have a room full
today! Hello ladies" Sam greeted as she entered Amora's
office.

"Hey Ms. Samantha" They greeted back.

"What's wrong?" Amora asked her.

"Mrs. Gionna is on the phone for you, she said she called
your cell and you didn't answer. She also told me to tell
you and whoever you are ignoring her for that she has a

cane and she will crack you and them with it" Sam told her relaying Mrs. Gionna's message causing everyone to laugh.

"I cannot wait to meet her, she is my type of lady" Sierra said in between laughs.

"Thank you Sam, I'll get it in here." Amora told her as she walked over to her desk and picked up the phone.

"Hey Gi, is everything okay?" Amora asked her.

"No, why do I have call all of these numbers to get you on the phone?" Mrs. Gionna fussed on the other end of the phone.

"I'm sorry Gi, I was in a session with a group of students, I didn't hear my cell ringing" Amora apologized.

"Are you okay?" Mrs. Gionna asked concerned.

"Yes what made you ask me that?" Amora replied "Gi don't tell me the reason you fussing at me is because you had another dream" Amora added.

"Yes the hell it is, are you sure you're okay? You don't need to talk to me about anything?" Mrs. Gionna pressed.

"No Gi, I'm fine! I promise and I will call you as soon as I get home. I have to wrap up this session for the day then I am getting out of here and you will have all of my attention. Is that cool with you?" Amora asked her.

"Yeah and your ass better call me back or I am getting on a plane and I am not playing Amora because I know you're lying to me about being okay" Mrs. Gionna told her.

"Two hours tops Gi and if I am not on your line in two hours I will book a flight for you myself" Amora reasoned.

"And it better be first class, talk to you in a minute" Mrs. Gionna told her then hung up.

"She does not play" Monae said causing the other girls to laugh.

"No she does not! Grown and all she will still try to beat me if I get out of line" Amora told them shaking her head and walking back over to them.

"Welp girls that is it for today" Amora said. "Don't look at me like that, I promise we will pick back up Monday after school" She added.

"That's a whole two days away Ms. Amora! What are we supposed to do until then?" Sierra complained

"You girls have to wait, I have to get home and so do you" Amora told them as she looked down at her watch.

"We don't have to get home, our folks don't care what we do" Monae said.

"Well I care that you make it home safely, the story will still be the same on Monday girls relax" Amora told them.

"Why can't we just come home with you?" Sierra asked.

"How about this, tomorrow we can have a girl's day? I'll open my office up and we will order pizza and I will finish telling the story, how does that sound?" Amora reasoned.

"That'll work! Tomorrow at 9am I will be here!" Monae said as she grabbed her bag.

"9am girl that's too early! How about 1:30pm and you girls can stay and chill with me all day" Amora told them.

"Cool" They shrugged and replied in unison then walked out of Amora's office. Once they were gone, Amora closed up her office and made her way home. After showering and slipping into a pair of tights and tank top, Amora grabbed her phone and dialed Mrs. Gionna.

"I am currently packing my bag, what time is my flight?" Mrs. Gionna spoke as soon as she answered the phone.

"Gi I'm five minutes late! If you wanted to come visit me that's all you had to say" Amora replied laughing.

"I miss you! You never have time for my old ass anymore" Mrs. Gionna told her sadly.

"Awe Gi I'm sorry. Tomorrow I promised my students a girl's day at my office but I promise I will change my flight and come to you tomorrow night" Amora promise.

"Alright baby! What's bothering you?" Mrs. Gionna asked.

"Even miles away you still can feel when I'm bothered" Amora chuckled.

"That's because you're my baby. Now talk to your Gi" Mrs. Gionna told her.

"I just feel a little emotional with telling my story to the girls and debating if I want to respond to my mother or not!

I don't hate her and you know that Gi but I am in a great space and I don't want her to take me back to a place that I fought hard as hell to move on from" Amora expressed.

"She can only take you where you allow her! The fact that she reached out after all these years is very questionable but I am sure it's for a reason. What are you really afraid of Amora?" Mrs. Gionna asked her.

"Turning back into that scared little girl I once was." Amore replied.

"This is where your faith comes in baby! God brought you through a lot, some of which you didn't even think he was present through but he was and he brought you through. Pray and ask that he cover every part of you and block anything that is not of him. You will be fine" Mrs. Gionna told her.

"Can you pray with me" Amora asked her letting tears escape from her eyes.

"Father in the name of Jesus, I lift Amora up to you right now and come against any ounce of fear and doubt she may possess. Father you've remained faithful to your word and brought her through every attack the enemy sent her way. I ask that you wrap your arms around her and embrace her with your presence. Strengthen her mind and give her peace with her mother. God we lift Stephanie up to you and ask that you deliver the hurt that she is carrying, give her peace with her past so that she is able to give Amora the love only a mother can give. Father I've done my best and all you've asked of me so I thank you for keeping Amora

and we claim victory in Jesus name, Amen!" Mrs. Gionna said as she ended her prayer.

"Amen! Thank you Gi, I needed that so bad" Amora replied.

"I know baby! If you want me to I will go with you to meet with your mother. You know she don't mess with my old ass, I done crack her upside her head too many times" Mrs. Gionna said causing Amora to laugh.

"You ain't ever lied about that" Amora said in between laughs. "Gi I love you lady" She added.

"I love you more! You feel better?" Mrs. Gionna asked.

"Yes Gi, I'm all better" Amora replied smiling into the phone.

"Good! Well I love you and I will see you tomorrow night God's willing. Have a good night baby" Mrs. Gionna told her.

"I love you more and make sure you have my Alfredo ready" Amora replied.

"Okay see you later" Mrs. Gionna said and hung up the phone. Removing the phone from her hear Amora sighed and snuggled under covers to get some much needed sleep.

The next day Amora walked in her office feeling a lot better than the day before so she decided to reply to her mother's email.

To: Stephanie Smith

Hello Mom, thank you for reaching out and I apologize
for being hesitant with my reply. I accept your
invitation to come and visit you, I will be in Philly
next week so I will make sure that I come see you.
Mrs. Gionna wants you to know that she will be
attending as well. Hope you are doing well.

See you soon, Amora

Closing her computer Amora sat back in her chair and silently prayed that her mother had actually changed and the visit would put them in a better place. Her prayer was interrupted by the bell ringing. After checking her watch for the time, Amora wondered who could be ringing the bell on a Saturday because she wasn't expecting the girls for another hour and a half. She couldn't help but laugh when she checked the camera and seen that it was the exact people she wasn't expecting until later.

"I could have sworn I told you girls 1:30" Amora said as she opened the door.

"You did but we knew you would be here early! You know because you practically live in your office and we were bored so we decided to come and keep you company earlier than expected" Monae smiled and walked passed Amora with the rest of the girls following.

"Hey Ms. Amora you look good girl" Sierra complimented playfully.

"Someone is in a good mood today" Amora complimented back.

"I am, I feel good today and I'm happy as hell to be spending it here with you" Sierra told her as they walked into Amora's office.

"Look at yall, all smiling and what not! This is what I like to see. I assume all of you had a good night?" Amora asked.

"Hell yeah because all we could think about was coming here today! We were all texting about it all night" Monae replied causing Amora to give her the eyes. "My fault, Heck yeah, is that better?" She added

"Much better" Amora told her. "Did you guys eat or are you hungry?" Amora asked.

"Yes we are!" They replied in unison.

"Pizza and wings okay?" Amore inquired.

"Yes and a cheesesteak please" Sierra added causing Amora to look her way.

"What the hell you know about a cheesesteak? I've been in Atlanta for a few years and haven't had a cheesesteak worthy of getting again especially because I'm from the home of the real Philly cheesesteaks" Amora said to them.

"They taste fine to me" Sierra shrugged. "I would like mines with extra mayo and ketchup please" She added.

"Anything else Princess" Amora asked sarcastically.

"French fries with a lot of ketchup" Sierra replied causing Monae to look her way and give her a warning look.

"Hungry much" Amora said to her.

"I didn't eat last night" Sierra lied quickly.

"Right" Amora replied. "I'll be right back let me go and order this food." Amora told them as she walked away with the phone to her ear.

"You better chill out before she figures it out" Monae warned.

"I can't help it, I'm so hungry" Sierra whispered as Amora pulled her chair in front of the couch the girls were sitting on.

"So do you girls just want to have regular chat until the food gets here so there won't be any interruptions?" Amora asked.

"Absolutely not, can you just get back to the story and when the food comes we can take a break to eat?" Sierra suggested.

"Okay so let me see where did I stop?" Amora spoke as she gathered her thoughts. "Okay so I always wrote how I was feeling in my diary and the day after leaving Gi's house was no different" Amora began.

Past

Diary Entry #3

Life is about living not dying

Life is about happiness and love after experiencing pain and hurt

Life is about chasing dreams not letting them die

Life is about overcoming hardships

Life is a value

Life should be treasured not taken for granted…

My life sucks and as much as I really don't want to be here I can't give up! Gi's words keep playing in my head "everything you're going through is for a purpose so that your story can inspire others going through the same thing". She can't possibly think I would actually tell people what happened to me. Not only is it embarrassing but it's shameful and it makes me feel so dirty every time I think about it. It makes me sick to my stomach replaying the numerous times my mother beat me so I was unrecognizable or when she tried to drown me or when she just hauled off and punched me in the face because someone called me pretty. Is my mom jealous of me? What would she have to be jealous about? I came from her, she created me so if she wants to blame anyone for the way I look she should be pointing the finger at herself. Being treated *the way I have been over the years makes me cringe every time someone calls me pretty or beautiful. It automatically makes me look over my shoulder anticipating a flying fist to connect to either my jaw or my eye. I wish I was able to embrace my beauty instead of shying away from it. I wonder if I will ever be comfortable with myself enough to accept my looks and own them.*

"Amora unlock this door!" My mother yelled as she twisted the door knob breaking me from my thoughts. After closing and hiding my diary, I jumped off of my bed and unlocked my bedroom door.

"Hey Mom" I spoke dryly.

"What are you in here doing?" She asked.

"Nothing I just woke up!" I told her rubbing my eyes.

"Well get dressed I have some meeting at the church!" She told me.

"Do I really have to go? Can't I just stay here?" I asked.

"No now do what I said and get dressed Amora, don't make me tell you again" She told me before walking out of the room.

"She is really beginning to get on my nerves" I mumbled to myself as I began to get dressed.

"You're not going to wash up or brush your hair?" She asked disgusted by my appearance. I was wearing a pair of baggy jeans with an oversized t-shirt, some sandals with my hair all over my head.

"Nope" I replied nonchalantly.

"You make me sick!" She told me.

"Yeah you told me that already!" I told her not backing down.

"Who are you talking to?" She asked standing to her feet and walking over to me.

"Nobody!" I replied walking out the front door, leaving her standing there.

"You better watch your mouth, that little attitude you got today is going to get you hurt!" My mother threatened walking behind me. Without responding, I climbed in the car and put my seat belt on. "Amora do you hear me fucking talking to you?" She asked me.

"Yes, I hear you mom!" I told her.

"Well act like it" She yelled as she pulled out the parking spot and headed to the church. "When we get in here lose your attitude Amora, nobody did anything to you today so get it together" She said to me.

"Okay mom!" I chuckled. I wasn't quite sure what was going on but I was not backing down from mother. I knew my smart remarks could possibly get me beat up but I really didn't care. I was fed up with my mother and how she treated me, I felt there wasn't much more she could do to me at this point besides kill me, everything else was done already.

"Is it okay if I sit out here while you handle your meeting?" I asked planning to go to Mrs.Gionna's house.

"Yeah after you come to speak to Pastor Damien" She told me getting out the car.

"Why do I have to speak to him? He won't even know I'm here because I'm not going to come in at all" I asked her as I closed the car door.

"Because I fucking said so" She replied punching me in the mouth. "I told you that mouth of yours was going to get you hurt, now stop playing with me you hear me?" She screamed standing over top of me. She hit me so hard I lost my balance.

"Now why the hell would you go and do that?" Mrs. Gionna yelled as she swung her cane at my mother. "I should clock you in your shit again!" She threatened before bending over and helping me to my feet. "You okay baby girl?" She asked me looking at my busted lip.

"First of all this is my daughter and I can do what I want to do to her. Second mind your business! And where did you even come from that fast?" My mother replied holding the spot on her head where Mrs. Gionna hit her and looked around confused.

"She is my business and I'm not going to sit around and keep watching you beat on her for no reason" Mrs. Gionna told her.

"Amora you told this nosey ass lady that I beat on you?" My mother asked me.

"No no, I haven't told her anything!" I stuttered and lied.

"So what is she talking about?" She asked moving closer to me.

"That's close enough!" Mrs. Gionna told my mother holding her cane out to block her from getting closer to me.

"I don't know mom!" I told her backing away slightly.

"She didn't tell me anything, I see everything you fucking devil. I saw you beat and stomp her and I just seen you punch her in the mouth for no damn reason" Mrs. Gionna told her stating facts. "If you don't want people in your business stop doing shit for everybody to see. How the hell would you like it if somebody just hauled off and punched you?" She asked. "Don't answer that, because you're going to find out if I see you lay a finger on her again" She threatened.

"Yeah whatever lady, Amora let's go!" My mother said before walking in the church.

"Gi why did you do that?" I asked as soon as my mother was out of sight.

"What did you expect me to do Amora? Sit across the street and do nothing?" Mrs. Gionna asked.

"Yes, I mean no. Man I don't know but I do know she is about to go crazy thinking I told you everything that has happened" I told her with fear my voice.

"What are you afraid of Amora?" Mrs. Gionna asked me.

"Her killing me" I told her with seriousness.

"Kill? Over my old wrinkled body" Mrs. Gionna shouted.

"Didn't I say come on Amora?" My mother asked walking back outside and interrupting our conversation.

"I'm coming, see you later Gi!" I told her before walking into the church.

"You make sure you stay away from that nosey lady you hear me?" My mother told me as she gripped me up by the collar of my shirt.

"Yes, I hear you!" I replied frustrated.

"Good, now Pastor Damien is looking for you" She told me. "Come on" She added before walking towards the back of the church. Wondering what he could possibly want with me in the back of the church, I began to worry. Following close behind my mother, I stopped once Pastor Damien came into view standing in front of a car covered with a sheet.

"Well hello there beautiful!" He greeted with a smile.

"Hey" I replied dryly.

"I'm sure your mom told you I was looking for you" He began. "I bought myself a new gift and I wanted to share it with you" He said smiling.

"Why?" I asked confused.

"Because I value you and I want your opinion on my new toy!" He replied.

"How much of an opinion can I give you?" I asked him.

"You can give me any kind of opinion you want beautiful!" Damien told me. "Especially because in just three short years you will be my wife" He added.

"Your what?" I asked making sure I heard him right.

"My wife" He repeated confidently. "Isn't that right Stephanie?" He said including my mother in the conversation.

"That's right daddy!" She replied with a fake smile plastered on her face.

"Yall both are nuts and even crazier than I thought if you think for a second I am marrying you when I turn 18." I spat angrily.

"You don't have a choice Amora, you don't have anybody else but me so what I say goes!" My mother said to me coming to Damien's defense.

"Now that we have that squared away, let me show you my new toy finally!" Damien smiled as he pulled the sheet off of his new all black Range Rover. "So what you think beautiful? She's almost as pretty as you. Want to go for a ride with me?" He asked as he climbed into the driver's seat.

"No I do not and your car is really ugly just like the both of you!" I told them before walking back inside the church. I had to get away from both of them, I felt like I was in the twilight zone or something. Was my mother serious? Was this a joke? How is this okay? I thought to myself as I ran up Mrs. Gionna's steps and began to bang on the door. "Gi open the door!" I yelled.

"What's wrong with you little girl?" Mrs. Gionna asked her as she held the door open for me to come in.

"Gi this can't be life" I chuckled "Like this has to get better right? Because right now I'm so confused! I'm lost, my life just doesn't make sense" I vented.

"Wait baby what are you talking about?" Mrs. Gionna asked as she sat down next to me on the couch.

"My mother, that damn Pastor they are two extremely sick individuals. Gi he just told me that my mother gave him her consent to marry me once I turn eighteen. First of all, that's impossible right? Because once I'm eighteen I can make my own decisions like I'm grown as long as I'm not living under her roof? Please tell me that's how it goes" I cried.

"Baby once you're eighteen and out of her house she has no control over you or your life" Mrs. Gionna informed me. "But wait where was that heffa at when he was saying all of this?" She asked.

"Right there Gi, with the fakest smile sitting on her face but fire in her eyes. She really does any and everything to make that pervert happy. Gi he could tell her to get up in front of the congregation completely naked and she would drop all of her clothes and do it not caring how she looked in front of all of those people like it's sad" I confessed.

"That man must have a golden penis" Mrs. Gionna stated seriously.

"Really" I asked giving her the side eye.

"Oh don't mind me chile, I was just thinking out loud" Mrs. Gionna replied flagging me. "Amora listen to me, the only way to put an end to this is to allow me to do something. You have to let me get the police involved, that's the only way I can get you away from them" She stated.

"No Gi you can't. What if the police can't do anything? What if they don't believe me? She is a really good liar, she can talk her way out of anything I've seen her do it plenty of times. I go to the police and once she is able to lie her way out of it she is going to come after me with so much force she may really kill me Gi I know she will" I told her through tears.

"You're really terrified that she is going to kill you aren't you?" Mrs. Gionna asked me.

"Yes Gi you don't see the look in her eyes when she beats on me. I see hatred; I see how much she means it when she says she wish I would just die already. When she says she hates me and hates all the attention I get. She is really determined to ruin my self-esteem she doesn't want me to be beautiful. I came from her how can she hate me so much? And why in the world would she ever tell that man a grown man that he can marry me?" I cried.

"Amora baby listen to me, you have to stand up for yourself. You want this to stop, we can figure out a way that you're comfortable with to stop this and get you far away from both of them. You know Gi got your back whichever way you decide to deal with this situation. But something has to be done soon before it's too late" Mrs. Gionna warned. "If it's as bad as you say it is and I believe it is, I can only imagine how worse it is when you're behind closed doors. We have to put an end to it. I can put an end to it right now if you want me to, all I have to do is go upstairs and grab my best friend and walk my ass right across the street. They would never see it coming" She told me referring to her gun she had stashed upstairs.

"No Gi, I don't want you to kill them! I don't want them dead, I just want them as far away from me as possible" I told her.

"You're so special baby you know that! Despite everything you've been through you still manage to have nothing but love in your heart. I've never seen anything like it because my ass would be on a rampage. I would have smothered your mother in her sleep if I was you and that damn Pastor, oh baby I would have a field day torturing his ass" Mrs. Gionna smiled wickedly.

"No matter how hard I try I just can't Gi. I'm hurt, I'm angry and embarrassed by the things that have happened to me but I can't find it in myself to hate either of them. I don't even want to do anything bad to them they will get what's coming to them eventually." I said to her.

"Yeah and I'm going to be the one to give them exactly what they need!" Mrs. Gionna threatened.

"Gi you're so crazy" I chuckled and wiped my tears away.

"Crazy about my baby, you know Gi loves you and always will" Mrs. Gionna said pulling me in for a hug then kissing my forehead.

Diary Entry #4

The only light in my life right now is Gi, she is the only reason I look forward to anything. My life is hard; it sucks it's depressing. Is it supposed to be this hard for me so young? I keep thinking about my mom telling Damien we could get married that had to have been a joke. What is it about that man that she willing to give me away just to keep him around? I actually thought about putting a pillow over my mother's face last night! I think Gi crazy self is rubbing off on me. I hate that those thoughts even consumed my mind she's my mother I'm not supposed to have these evil feeling or thoughts towards her. But can you blame me? I didn't ask my dad to leave hell I didn't ask her to have me she decided to so why am I being punished? I will never understand. The day the conversation happened, I was scared but happy at the same time that Gi clocked my mom in the head. Gi crazy self didn't care that she wasn't a match for my mom physically, she was defending me and I love her so much for that. Nobody ever defends me, everyone just sits around and pretends not to see what is going on. Not Gi she not playing no games, before meeting Gi I felt like I didn't have anyone well besides my sister and best friend but I now know what it feels like to have someone who genuinely loves and care about you. I just need to get as far away from my mom and Damien as possible.

The next morning just as I was finishing another diary entry I heard my mother call out for me. "Amora are you up?" She screamed from her room breaking me from my thoughts.

"Yeah I'm about to get dressed now!" I replied while putting my diary back in its hiding spot and climbing out of bed. Grabbing my towel and shower cap I went to take a shower. After showering, washing my hair and brushing my teeth, I grabbed my things and exited the bathroom.

"Good morning beautiful" Damien greeted walking out of my mother's room.

"Hi" I replied gripping my towel tightly and walking around him.

"See you in service." He chuckled.

Rolling my eyes, I slammed my door making sure to lock it before dropping my towel. Looking through my drawer I searched for something comfortable to wear to church because I knew we were going to be there all day due to it being Damien's anniversary of him becoming a Pastor. I didn't understand why they were honoring a man who wasn't living by the world of God, he was a big fraud.

"Amora I told you about slamming doors in my house. I'm not gone tell you again" My mother yelled.

"*Yeah whatever, you all late*" I mumbled low enough so she couldn't hear me. Deciding on a pink sundress and a pair of sandals, I put my hair in a bun then put favorite diamond studs in my ears. I couldn't help but smile thinking back to when I was once a happy girl and my father surprised me with the diamond earrings.

"How's my favorite girl"? My father smiled walking into the house and over to me.

"Good daddy", I giggled and hugged him.

"I brought you a present baby girl. Want to see what it is?" He said to me.

"Yes!" I screamed with excitement.

"Okay come on walk me outside to the car" My father told me and led the way. Following behind my father, I felt like the luckiest girl in the world, I loved when my father surprised me with gifts. He wasn't home a lot so I didn't get much attention but when he was home he made up for the time he missed. "Okay close your eyes baby" He told me once we reached the car. Doing as I was told, I closed my eyes then extended my hand.

"Close your hand Amora" My father chuckled and removed a small box from the bag and opened it. "Okay baby girl open your eyes" He told me.

Popping my eyes open, I screamed and jumped up and down. "Dad they are so pretty, can I wear them now?" I asked him.

"Of course let me put them on for you" He replied as he removed the earrings from the box and put them in my ears.

"I brought all of you a pair but yours are special Amora, I had your initials engraved around the crown of them. I'm not around a lot but don't ever think daddy isn't thinking of you wishing I could be around more. I have to provide for us so you all don't want for anything" My father explained.

"I know daddy and thank you for my gift, I love them I'm going to wear them all of the time." I told him.

"I love you baby girl. I'll always be here for you" He assured me.

"I love you too" I responded and kissed his cheek

"Amora are you ready?" My mother asked me interrupting my thoughts.

"Yeah" I replied clearing my throat and wiping the tears from my eyes. Not only didn't my father keep his promises but he also acted as if I meant absolutely nothing to him. How could he go so long without making sure I was okay or speaking to me? How could he just get married and forget he has another daughter other than Sionni. If my own parents didn't care about me how was I supposed to believe other people did? Yeah Gi showed me nothing but love and affection that I've been yearning for but would it stop? Will she eventually forget about me too? All of these thoughts invaded my mind as I grabbed my bag then left my room.

"Go ahead and get in the car, I have to grab something" My mother told me as she walked back up the steps.

"Okay" I replied grabbing the car keys and walking out of the house.

Moments later my mother got in the car, started it and pulled off without saying a word. Her silence towards me wasn't anything out of the ordinary to so I leaned my head back and stared out the window the entire ride to the church. Fifteen minutes later we were pulling up to the church, I couldn't help but smile when I saw Mrs. Gionna sitting on her porch as usual with her cane and her dog talking trash to the members of the church who always sat on her steps. Laughing to myself, I thought back to when I asked Mrs. Gionna why she hated the church so much.

"Gi, why you always cursing the people that go the church out?" I asked Mrs. Gionna.

"Because I can't stand them brain washed heffa's nor that devil of a Pastor they listen to" She replied with anger in her voice.

"But what did they do to you though Gi?" I asked "if they want to be "brainwashed" as you call it that's their problem not yours. Why do you care?" I added.

"Because my dummy of a daughter is one of those brainwashed heffa's and that little dummy stopped speaking and coming to see me because that damn Pastor told her I was too nosey and nothing but the devil after I pulled my gun out on him one time I walked in on his ass beating on her." Mrs. Gionna fussed.

"Gi you mean to tell me all this time you had a daughter and never told me about her?" I asked in disbelief. "I thought we told each other everything, you been keeping secrets and I don't like it!" I told her.

122

"She disowned me, I never disowned her! I just choose not to talk about it. You're never supposed to go against family for no man because when he decides to leave family will still be there" Mrs. Gionna began *"I can't tell you the last time I spoke to my daughter I see her very often but she walks by me like I didn't give birth to her bald head ass."* She cursed *"I do tell your little sneaky ass everything although you've been keeping something from me. I should knock you in your shit"* Mrs. Gionna fussed while lifting her cane and pretending to swing it at me.

"Wait what? How you turn this around on me?" I asked ducking my head so she wouldn't hit me.

"When were you going to tell me about that little girl you been texting and calling?" Mrs. Gionna asked her.

"Huh?" I asked choking on the water I was drinking. *"Gi come on now how do you know about that?"* I asked her.

"I know everything sneaky and besides you left the messages open last week when you fell asleep on the couch so I took that as you wanting to share them with me" Mrs. Gionna replied innocently.

"Gi you're so nosey." I chuckled. *"But what's your daughter's name? Does she still go to the church?"* I asked changing the subject.

"Yeah her stupid ass still goes there, her name is Joseline" Mrs. Gionna told me.

"Wait I know her!" I said. *"Now that I think about it yall look a lot alike."* I added.

"Duh Amora, she is my daughter!" Mrs. Gionna replied smartly.

"Whatever Gi" I said rolling her eyes. "She's nosey just like you too, she always telling me I can talk to her and calling me beautiful and stuff. Stephanie always tells me to stay away from her though." I told her.

"I bet she do, they both messing around with that damn Pastor so they don't like each other. But don't you tell that daughter of mines anything. She is wicked just like that mother of yours." Mrs. Gionna warned. "Now back to that pretty girl you've been texting" She joked.

"Dang Gi you went that far back in the messages to when she sent a picture?" I asked.

"Yup now get to talking." Mrs. Gionna laughed and told me.

"Earth to Amora" My mother yelled breaking me from my thoughts.

"Huh? I'm sorry mom what did you say?" I asked confused.

"I said come on! You want to be staring off into space and shit! Get your dumb ass out the car" She demanded. Remaining quiet I got out the car and walked towards the church. With my mother walking a few feet ahead of me and stopping to speak to the many church members who were gathered in front of the church, I took the opportunity to sneak off to Mrs. Gionna's.

"Hey Gi" I sang as I walked up her step.

"Hey my baby, I saw you and that devil drive up!" Mrs. Gionna told me.

"Of course you did Gi! I saw you out here cursing them too" I laughed.

"Yeah them damn heathens always parking their asses on my property as if I like them. You know I can't stand them church folks" She replied frustrated.

"I know Gi, I just came to say hi before I went inside. I'm going to try to sneak away at some point during the day because it's three services today. Can you make me some Alfredo please?" I asked cheesing, hoping she would say yes.

"Of course baby! I'll see you later" Mrs. Gionna said as she watched me walk back down the steps and across the street to the church.

Present

Amora's story was interrupted by the ringing of her phone. "Excuse me, it's probably the deliver guy" Amora said as she stopped the story and rushed to answer her phone.

"Hello" She answered. "Okay I'll be right out!" Amora confirmed before grabbing her wallet and leaving her office.

"Yall what if Ms. Amora is our Mrs. Gionna?" Monae said as she turned and faced her friends. "Think about it Mrs. Gionna saw something in Ms. Amora that she didn't even see in herself which is why she was so drawn to her. Ms. Amora is pushing us to greatness because she believes in us as young women but what if she can help us personally as well?" Monae finished excitingly.

"Only time will tell" Sierra replied as Amora walked back in the office carrying the food. Sierra and Monae both got up to help with all the things she had piled in her hands.

"I cannot wait to eat, I'm so hungry!" Sierra confessed.

"I can't either, I went straight to sleep last night and didn't bother eating anything I was so tired!" Amora countered. An hour later, the food was completely gone and Amora and all of her students were full and happy.

"That hit the spot huh?" Amora asked them.

"Let me find out Ms. Amora got a little hood in her." Monae teased.

"Oh it's definitely in me! I just know when to turn it on and when to turn it off but I always keep it 100" Amora told them.

"I feel that vibe sis" Sierra expressed snapping her fingers causing Amora to laugh.

"Anyway after walking away from Gi I joined my mother inside the church for service" Amora said as she got back into the story.

Past

"Today we celebrate a great man of God, a man who is generous, a man who is faithful not only to the people of God but to God himself, a man who is a walking testimony of the gospel of Christ. That man is none other than Pastor Damien West himself. I've known this man for ten some odd years, see I'm not going to tell yall the exact number of years because then I would be telling my age." The guest preacher joked causing the congregation to erupt in laughter. "Damien is my brother we speak often and hold each other secrets tightly, he knows if he ever needs me I'm coming no questions asked. I'm so proud of you and all of the work you've done here at this wonderful church and I am excited for where God is about to lead you." He continued before stopping and looking at Pastor Damien then the congregation. "I'm sorry Damien but I have to stop here, the spirit is putting something on my heart that I cannot ignore. I'm not one to put people on the spot because I really dislike when it's done to me but when the Holy Spirit speaks I must obey. I'm opening the altar right now, there is someone in this place who is extremely broken they feel like they've been calling on God and he has not showed up. They feel like they have nowhere to turn or how to get out of the situation they are in, if that is you I want you to come up here right now! I would like to pray with you" He spoke to the congregation. "You do not have to be afraid, he hears your cries and he wants me to tell you that it's going to get better" He added "I need you to come up here with me right now! I am trying to give you the opportunity before I come and get you" He spoke "You there with the bun, sitting in the second row" He pointed "I need you to come up here with me right now!" He said causing everyone to look around to see who he was referring to. "The young girl with the pink dress looking down at the floor, I am talking to you" He declared causing me to look up.

"Not again!" I thought to myself. There was no way I was about to be embarrassed in front of the church for the second time. *"Is he talking me? He can't be talking to me; he doesn't even know me!"* I thought to myself as I looked around.

"No need to look around sweetie, I am indeed talking to you! I need you to join me up here at this alter" He spoke "Do you want me to come get you?" He asked causing everyone to continue to look around wondering who he was talking to. "You're taking too long and this cannot wait" He said and walked over to me extending his hand for me to take it.

"This is really happening again!" I mumbled to myself as I accepted the preacher's hand and rose from my seat.

"It's okay young lady no need to be scared I am not going to hurt you I am trying to help you!" He began "What's your name?" He asked me.

"Amora" I replied with my head down.

"Hello Amora, I am Pastor Cater, I've been preaching for over fifteen years and I can honestly count on both hands how many times the spirit spoke to me so directly to me

128

about a person that I was able to directly point them out. Usually it's general and people who can relate will come up for prayer but you my dear, God wanted me to get some things clear to you. He hears your cries and he wants you to know that he is with you, he need you to trust him. Who are you here with?" He asked.

"My mom" I told him.

"Mom I need you to come up here!" Pastor Carter spoke while looking into the congregation as my mother made her way to the altar.

"Hi Mom" He spoke.

"Hello Pastor" She spoke and began to stroke my hair.

"This baby is in danger! The person you have her around is preying on her, I'm not sure if you are aware or just oblivious to this but you need to protect her. Her purpose in life is far too great for her to be damaged before she gets a chance to live her truth. Everyone bow your heads. *Father we come to you as humble as we know how, God I lift this young girl up to you father, I ask that you protect her that you guide her that you live through her so that she see the potential of greatness you've instilled in her. Father open her mother's eyes to see this precious gift she birthed, allow her to nurture her the right way, to love her the right way, to protect her the right way. Father God give Amora the strength to fight and be strong through the many battles she is facing father God to know that her reward is far more greater than what she is fighting right now. Father wrap your loving arms around her and give her the security she needs to know that you're with her every step of the way. I ask you all these things and declare them done in Jesus*

name, and all the people of God shout Amen" He finished.
"Lift your head young lady! You don't ever walk around
with your head down. You're the daughter of a king who
can do things beyond your imagination you just have to
trust him." He told me and wiped the tears that stained my
face. Burying my head in his chest, I cried. Not because I
was embarrassed but because I was now convinced that
God was finally hearing my cries and was going to rescue
me. How else could a complete stranger pick me out of a
room full of people and run down almost everything I was
going through.

"It's okay sweetie, your breakthrough is coming!" Pastor
Carter assured me. "Mom you take care of her more
carefully, protect her you hear me?" He said my mother.

"Yes, Pastor" She replied forcing tears to fall from her eyes
causing me to cut my eyes at her then at Damien.

"Please listen to me and listen good! I can't stress this
enough God has wonderful things planned for her. This girl
is destined for greatness please don't allow her to be
harmed by your inability to pay attention to the danger you
allow around her and yourself" He told my mother. "You
two may return to your seats now!" He said to us finally
letting me go then kissing my forehead. Unable to stop my
tears, I asked my mother if I could be excused, not really
having a choice but to agree she shook her head yeah and
allowed me to leave the church. Once outside I wasted no
time running straight to Mrs. Gionna's house not bothering
to knock, I walked straight through the door and ran
straight into her arms.

"What's the matter Amora?" She asked. Wiping my face, I picked my head up and told Mrs. Gionna everything that just happened in church. "Gi, out of everybody in that church how would he know to pick me out? I'm so confused and I honestly don't know if my tears are due to me being scared, frustrated or relieved. I want to believe there is a God, I want to believe that at some point all of this will come to an end I really want to but when is it going to happen Gi" I asked.

"Listen if I were in your shoes I think I would be questioning all of the same things. I'm not the most religious person baby you know I have my ways but I do know God has a way of making his presence known and he speaks through his people so believe that if he pointed you out it were for a reason. You say you've never met him before right?" Mrs. Gionna asked.

"Right never seen that man a day in my life and of course my mom was up there faking as usual" I told her before rolling my eyes.

"Then baby maybe, just maybe this is what you've been praying for! Some type of sign that God hears your cries and he is going to show up when you least expect it" Mrs. Gionna expressed to me.

"I guess Gi. I don't know, the way I've been feeling lately I've just been really numb, like what she do and say to me anymore it's like okay I get it you hate me tell me something I don't know!" I explained to her.

"I really can't stand your mother Amora; I hate that she makes you feel this way. In spite all of that baby you know your Gi loves you. I have more than enough love to shower you with!" Mrs. Gionna said while smiling and wrapping her arms tightly around me.

"I know Gi and I love you too crazy lady" I smiled hugging her back.

"You better now come on, let me make you a plate because I know your greedy butt is hungry" Mrs. Gionna joked as she opened the pot and filled the plate with shrimp Alfredo and a piece of garlic bread then handed it to me.

"Thanks Gi" I said I grabbed the plate from her and sat at the table. "Gi I swear you make the best Alfredo" I complimented as I stuffed my mouth with food.

"You so damn silly girl" Mrs. Gionna laughed as she took a seat next to me and began to eat her food. "This is good though" She added.

"Gi can you put me some in a container so I can take some home with me?" I asked as I put my empty plate in the sink.

"Of course but what did you do swallow the damn food without chewing it Amora?" Mrs. Gionna joked.

"Leave me alone Gi, I was hungry" I laughed. "I should probably get back over to that church before my mom be outside acting crazy. You know she told me to stay away from you because you were nosey" I told her.

"I don't care what she told you I know you better not listen to her. I'm going to end up cracking your mother's shit to the white meat, she keeps testing me" Mrs. Gionna told me.

"Gi you're so violent!" I laughed.

"You know I don't play when it comes to my baby so I'll be violent I really don't care" Mrs. Gionna said to me.

"I love you Gi, I'm going to call you later before I go to sleep so you know that I'm okay" I told her as I walked towards the front door.

"I love you more Amora and okay don't forget because you know I will come to that house" Mrs. Gionna yelled after me.

"Amora didn't I tell you to stay away from that nosey lady?" My mother yelled once she noticed me leaving Mrs. Gionna house.

"Yeah but." I began but was cut off by my mother's fist. "What did you hit me for, I didn't even do anything?" I asked holding my eye.

"You don't listen I've been looking for you for over an hour and come to find out your hard headed ass was doing something I told you not to do" She screamed "Stop trying me Amora and don't get a boost of courage because of what that bulshit ass preacher said earlier, you know just like I do everything that happens to you is because I allow it and anything I don't want to happen to you won't. You got that?" She threatened.

"Clear as day!" I replied looking my mother in the eyes completely unfazed by what she was screaming at me.

"You can continue to say whatever you want to her but didn't I tell you not to raise your stinking hands and hit her again? I swear you're pushing my hand Satan" Mrs. Gionna threatened walking across the street.

"Its fine Gi, I'm okay!" I told her trying to avoid her from coming across the street.

"Shut up girl, no you're not! Let me see your eye" Mrs. Gionna told me finally reaching me and examining my eye.

"I'm only going to say this one more time, mind your business! That's my daughter and I can do anything I fucking want to her she is none of your concern. I've been trying to be nice but you're trying me with your nosey ass. Next time I'm going to forget you're an old lady and slap the shit out of you then I'm going to call the police because I told you to stay away from my daughter" My mother threatened.

"You can try to slap me and see where that gets you heffa, don't let this cane fool you. I walk around with it because I want to not because I need to. Now if you want to call the police be my guest hell I'll let you use my phone. But I'm sure you don't want to take that route with all secrets you have" Mrs. Gionna taunted with her hand on her hip.

"Omg Gi, that's enough can you please just go home?" I begged afraid of how this argument was going to end.

"I said my peace but you remember what I said I better not see you hit her again" Mrs. Gionna threatened with her cane pointed at my mother then walked back across the street.

"I'm not finished with you!" My mother threatened me never bothering to respond to Mrs. Gionna. *"Of course you're not!"* I mumbled and walked into the church.

One week later

"Omg Amora! Thank God you're awake!" Mrs. Gionna sighed a breath of relief once she saw my eyes pop open. Frantically looking around, I began to panic. Due to there being a tube down my throat I was unable to talk so I began to pull on the multiple cords that were connected to my body.

"Calm down baby! Let me go get the nurse hold tight!" Mrs. Gionna told me before leaving the room and returning a few minutes later with a nurse.

"Look who finally decided to join us! I know you're confused so I am going to take the tube out and give you some water because your throat is going to be sore. Then I will answer any questions you have okay sweetie" The nurse said to me.

"Be gentle lady!" Mrs. Gionna told the nurse standing behind her watching her every move. Once the tube was removed from my throat, I wasted no time guzzling the ice water the nurse handed me.

"You okay baby?" Mrs. Gionna asked taking the empty cup from me.

"I think so! How long have I been in here?" I asked running my hands through my wild hair.

"A little over a week" You've been unconscious since I brought you here. Amora baby do you remember everything that happened" Mrs. Gionna asked lying in the bed next to me. Allowing tears to fall, I shook my head yes and thought back to the night that landed me in the hospital.

Present

"Amora! Amora are you here?" Sam yelled frantically as she entered the building then ran into Amora's office.

"I'm right here Sam, what's wrong?" She asked her as she stood up from the chair she was sitting in.

"Why aren't you answering your phone? Sionni is trying to reach you. It has something to do with Mrs. Gionna" Sam told her causing Amora to panic.

"What about her? Is she okay?" Amora asked as she grabbed her phone and noticed all of the missed calls and text messages from Sionni and a number she didn't recognize. She decided to call Sionni back first.

"Amora you have to get here! It's Mrs. Gionna" Sionni said sadly when she answered the phone.

"What about her Sionni? Is she okay? Just tell me she's okay" Amora replied on the verge of tears.

"Sis please just come to Philly! Hurry" Sionni told her.

"I'm leaving now" Amora said before hanging up and checking the voicemail that popped up. *"Hello this message is for Amora Smith concerning Mrs. Gionna Boyd. She is currently admitted here at our hospital and things do not look good for her. We need someone to come down here as soon as possible so that we are able to speak to them on her behalf, she isn't conscious. Please give us a call at your earliest convenience."* The doctor said as he ended his message.

"Oh my god, I have to get out of here. I'm sorry girls but I have to go and check on my Gi. Umm Sam can you please make sure they get home safely. I'm going straight to the airport" Amora told them as she rushed out of her office.

"Amora make sure you call me and Pray girl it's the only thing you can do until you make it there" Sam yelled out as Amora ran out of the building. Jumping in her car and speeding off, Amora silently prayed that Mrs. Gionna would be strong and pull through and that she didn't run into the horrific Atlanta traffic as she rushed to the airport. Making it to the airport in record time, Amora parked her car in the garage and jumped on the shuttle to go to the terminal. Because the flight she purchased previously wasn't scheduled to leave for another five hours, Amora walked up to the ticket agent and purchased a ticket for the next flight leaving out. After going through security and making her way to her gate Amora did the only thing she felt she could do at the moment. She dropped to her knees and called on the only person she knew could get her through what she was dealing with. *"God you said to call on you in our time of need so I'm coming to you right now asking that you spare Gi's life. Father she has been my rock for so long, I can't lose her. I know you make no mistakes, I just ask that you wrap your arms around her and give her the strength to stick around and that you give me strength to be strong like she taught me. Father I need you because I am an emotional wreck allow me to trust you. I pray that you give me travel mercy as I get on this plane and that you allow Gi to still be around when I get there. In Jesus name Amen"* Amora finished her prayer and got off of her knees and sat back in her chair waiting for her flight to board. After boarding and settling in her seat, Amora closed her eyes and allowed sleep to consume her. Two hours later she was being awakened by the flight attendant for her to exit the plane. Looking around her confused Amora realized that she had slept the entire flight and was the last one on board. Grabbing her pocketbook from under the seat, Amora rushed off of the airplane and out of the airport. While she waited for her Uber to arrive, Amora called the hospital to check on Mrs. Gionna again.

"University of Pennsylvania how may I direct your call?" The receptionist asked.

"Can I please be transferred to the ICU" Amora requested.

"Sure please hold" The receptionist told Amora then transferred the call. Moments later a nurse answered.

"ICU this is Amanda" The nurse spoke.

"Hi my name is Amora Smith, I was contacted in regards to my grandmother Mrs. Gionna Boyd I was calling to check on her status." Amora told her.

"Hold on one minute please" She replied while placing Amora on hold. Getting into her Uber, Amora patiently waited for the nurse to return to the phone.

"Umm Miss Smith, I am not allowed to give the patients status over the phone" The nurse said.

"Why not? You guys called and told me to give you a call then when I do you tell me you can't tell me anything over the phone? That makes no sense" Amora told her.

"Look I don't make the rules" The nurse replied ignorantly.

"Can I speak with someone else? Whoever is in charge?" Amore requested.

"I am the head nurse of the floor so I guess that would make me who you are requesting. And like I said it's against hospital policies to give patient status over the phone" She told Amora causing her to become frustrated and pinch the bridge of her nose.

"You know what, Fine" Amora replied then hung up angrily. *"God I need your strength please grant me patience so that when I get up there I don't snatch that nurse from behind that desk"* Amora mumbled as her Uber driver pulled up to the hospital. Gathering her belongings, Amora took a deep breathe then walked inside of the hospital and made her way up to the ICU. Getting off of the elevator, Amora followed the directions that lead her to Mrs. Gionna's room.

"Amora" Sionni screamed as she ran and embraced her sister.

"Si what happened? I just talked to her last night and she was fine" Amora told her as they walked towards the door.

"I don't know Amora, they would only tell me but so much because I am not listed as one of her emergency contacts. I was here visiting Tina, because she just had her baby and I saw them rushing Mrs. Gionna in on the gurney" Sionni told her sister. Bracing herself Amora opened the door and pulled the curtain back, unable to withstand the sight before her Amora dropped everything that was in her hands then ran over to Mrs. Gionna and broke down.

"Gi I need you to wake up, this is not you. You're not supposed to be laying here like this; I just talk to you last night. Why didn't you tell me you weren't feeling well?" Amora cried and bombarded with questions. Sionni knew that there was nothing she could say to make her sister feel better at the moment so she held her sister as she cried.

"Um excuse me I am Doctor Thomas, are you her granddaughter Amora?" The doctor asked as he grabbed tissues then handed them to Amora.

"Yes I'm Amora, I think you're the doctor that left the message on my phone. What is wrong with her?" Amora asked sniffling.

"Mrs. Gionna had a brain aneurysm, she knew about it for a while but she is a very stubborn woman and refused to let us operate. The aneurysm burst and her neighbor found her lying unconscious on the floor. Mrs. Gionna went an hour without oxygen to her brain which means the damage was already done before she got here and unfortunately there isn't much more we can do for her. She is not breathing on her own, the machine is breathing for her it's the only reason she is still laying there" Doctor Thomas told her sadly causing Amora to lose her balance.

"So what are you saying" Amora asked with tears streaming down her face.

"I'm sorry but we did all we could, there is nothing more we can do. She is brain dead and there is no coming back from that" He broke to Amora causing her scream and yell.

"NOO! There has to be something else you can do, I'll pay you whatever it will cost just please don't let her die Amora begged as she and Sionni both continued to cry.

"I'm sorry Amora but I'm afraid she is already gone. As I said the only keeping her hear is the machine." Doctor Thomas explained.

"God this cannot be happening to me! Gi you told me you would never leave me, you told me that you would always be here for me. Why would you leave me like this? I need you" Amora cried while holding Mrs. Gionna's hand and hugging Sionni. Walking over to Amora and Sionni, Doctor Thomas did something he doesn't normally do during situations like this.

"For some reason I cannot walk away and leave you like this. All she did was talk about her 'Amora'" He chuckled. "She was very proud of you and you brought so much joy to her life. She lived a very full and loving life and she instilled those same qualities she possessed inside of you. She may not be here physically for you anymore Amora, but she will forever be in your heart which means she goes wherever you go. This is sad because she is no longer with us but appreciate the memories you two did share and what she was able to teach you" Doctor Thomas expressed as he embraced them.

"I've never experience this type of hurt before because the person that helped me overcome anything that brought me any kind of pain was her. This shit hurt" Amora cried harder. Realizing it was best to just allow Amora to cry and vent, Doctor Thomas turned off his beeper and allowed Amora to cry it out. "I'm sorry, I wet your entire jacket with my tears and snot" Amora said moment s later as she took her tissue and attempted to wipe the mess she made on Doctor Thomas.

"I think I'm going to need a little more than some tissue to get this jacket clean" He joked. "Just joking, don't worry about it! You needed to cry and I allowed you to do just that" He told her.

"How much longer can you keep her on the machine?" Sionni asked looking over at Mrs. Gionna.

"Legally about another week! However I want you to be mindful that she will not come back from this." He replied.

"Okay we just want to try and contact her daughter so she can get a chance to say goodbye before you take her off of it" Sionni told him speaking for Amora.

"Okay that's fine! There are nurses at the station if you need anything and here is my card with my contact information call me if you need anything" Dr. Thomas told her.

"Okay thank you. Can I ask a question?" Amora asked.

"Sure" He told her.

"Is it your hospital's policy not to give patient updates to family members over the phone?" Amora asked him.

"No! As long as the family member that is calling is listed on the patient contact information we are entitled to disclose them with information because in some cases the family members are not able to get to the hospital right away. Why is that what someone at this hospital told you?" He asked her.

"No!" Amora lied. "Just wondering" She added. Although she was in the position to get the nurse who gave her a hard time over the phone in trouble, that was not her concern right now.

"Okay! You have my info, let me know if you need anything" Dr. Thomas told Amora as he walked towards the door.

"Okay, Thank you!" Amora told him as she looked around the room for her phone.

"Si have you seen my phone?" Amora asked her.

"Here" Sionni replied handing Amora her phone.

"I don't even remember giving it to" Amora chuckled and shook her head.

"You didn't! You damn near through it at me when you ran over to Mrs. Gionna bed" Sionna replied. "Do you have Joseline's number?" She asked Amora.

"Not on me. It's on my laptop that I left at my office. I'm going to call Sam to see if she can get it for me" Amora told her as she dialed Sam's number.

"Hey Bestie, how is she?" Sam asked as soon as she answered the phone.

"Not good, not good at all. She's gone" Amora cried into the phone.

"Oh my god! I'm so sorry, I'm coming to you. I am about to book me a flight right now" Sam assured her.

"I just wish I could hear her voice one last time Sam, I miss her so much already" Amora confessed as she continued to cry.

"I know you do bestie. What happened to her?" Sam asked.

"She had a brain aneurysm and refused to get operated on and it burst. It's nothing else they can do because she's brain dead" Amora sniffled.

"Damn Mrs. Gionna! Well I'm coming Amora, I am just leaving the office the girls suckered me into letting them stay and chill at the office but I am dropping them off right now. Then I am going to go home and grab a couple things and go to the airport. Alright?" Sam said to her.

"Ms. Amora we are so sorry to hear about Mrs. Gionna, and I know you probably don't want to hear this right now but you are going to be okay and everything is going to be fine. You know why?" Sierra yelled from the background.

"Why?" Amora whispered with tears in her eyes.

"Because we got your back" Sierra assured her as Monae and the other girls cosigned her. "God didn't bring you this far to leave you. Isn't that what you told me? He got you and we got you too" Sierra told Amora causing a flood of tears to escape from her eyes.

"I appreciate you girls so much" Amora told them.

"Mora, I'll call you when I get to the airport and let you know what flight I am on." Sam told Amora.

"Okay and when you get a chance can you send me Joseline's contact info off of my laptop? I need to get in contact with her and let her know what's going on" Amora replied.

"Yeah sure, I'll send it as soon as I stop when I drop them off" Sam assured her.

"Okay thank you! I will talk to you girls later, please stay out of trouble" Amora told them.

"We will and we will be seeing you soon Ms. Amora don't worry" Monae replied.

"Alight bye" Amora said before hanging up and walking back over to the bed Mrs. Gionna was lying in.

"I was not prepared for this Gi, What am I supposed to do?" Amora asked as she pulled a chair up to the bed and laid her head at Mrs. Gionna's feet. *"God I don't quite understand what you're doing but please give me clarity and peace to accept your will"* Amora mumbled as she allowed the tears to flow freely from her eyes. Amora cried so much that she never realized she cried herself to sleep until she was being awoken out of her sleep by someone crying.

"Ma I'm so sorry" Joseline cried while Sionni rubbed her back. Getting up from the chair she was sitting, Amora walked over to Joseline and embraced her. Although she knew what the relationship was like between Mrs. Gionna and her daughter Joseline, it didn't take away from the fact that Mrs. Gionna was in fact her mother and she had just lost her. "I remember when I was a little girl and I would get bullied in school for being so short. Ma came up to the school, you know she was short so they thought she was like an older cousin and she helped me fight every girl that ever bullied me" Joseline reminisced and chuckled causing Amora and Sionni to laugh.

"She did not play when it came to people she loved" Amora countered and smiled.

"At all and even despite how I treated her, and how many times I walked past her like she didn't raise me and no matter what I said to her she never allowed someone else to treat me wrong. Which is why Damien didn't like her" Joseline said laughing causing Amora to tense up a bit. "Oh I'm sorry Amora, I didn't mean to bring him up I was just in the moment" Joseline apologized.

"It's fine! How did you find out? I was going to call you" Amora told her.

"Dr. Thomas got in touch with me. He told me you were taking it pretty hard and didn't know if you had a chance to reach out to me. How are you holding up? I know how much Ma meant to you and you did no wrong in her eyes" Joseline said laughing and jokingly rolling her eyes at Amora.

"Mrs. Gionna did not play about her baby girl" Sionni added teasing Amora.

"Gi is my heart! I don't know what I am going to do without her" Amora said as she began to cry again.

"Exactly what she taught you to do and that's to live your life inspiring others with what you've been brought through. Amora listen, I never got a chance to tell you this but part of the reason why Damien got the punishment he did is because of me! I ummm" Joseline began but was interrupted by a group of doctors entering the room.

"Ms. Boyd I'm glad you were able to make it here. How are you ladies feeling giving the circumstances?" Dr. Thomas asked.

"Is everything okay?" Amora asked ignoring his question. She didn't mean to come off as rude but no matter how many times someone asked her if she was okay her answer was not going to change. She just lost the only mother figure she's known, no she was not okay.

"Yes, well I don't know how much you and Joseline had a chance to talk about but we need to know what you're decision is going to. Are you going to take her off today or do you wish to max out her days?" He asked them causing Amora and Joseline to look at each other.

"Today" They both replied in unison. It would be selfish of them to continue to have Mrs. Gionna hooked up to the machine because they weren't ready to let go. She was gone and it was better for them to begin preparing for her service then to continue to cry over her physical form, her spirit was no longer with them. Without responding the doctors signaled the nurses who began to take each tube out of Mrs. Gionna's body. Once every tube was out, Amora, Sionni and Joseline watched Mrs. Gionna's body move up and down on last time before the doctors called the time of death. *March 20, 2017 Mrs. Gionna Boyd* earned her wings.

"We have to send Ma off the right way" Joseline said breaking the silence. Amora stood there starring at Mrs. Gionna's lifeless body unable to move or speak. "Amora! Did you hear me?" Joseline asked looking at her. Frozen from shock, her reality finally sat in and caused her to suffer from a panic attack something she hasn't had in years. Amora began to hyperventilate, unable to catch her breath she started grasping her neck and stumbling backwards.

"She's having a panic attack! Get some help" Sionni yelled as she rushed to her sister's aide.

"Amora! Amora are you alright? Nurse! Doctor! Somebody come help" Joseline yelled frantically. "Amora I need you to relax sweetie and breathe. Take a deep breathe" Joseline attempted to coach her as Dr. Thomas and a nurse following him rushed inside of the room.

"Amora, it's Dr. Thomas, I need you to calm down and take a deep breath for me! I want you to follow after me. Inhale! Exhale deeply" He coached allowing Amora to follow. After several deep breathes Amora was able to regulate her breathing and relax. "There we go! Nurse get her a cup of water please" Dr. Thomas instructed.

"I sure do not miss dealing with that! Amora used to have those all of the time when we were younger" Sionni sighed.

"You scared the living shit out of me girl! Are you okay?" Joseline asked.

"You just sounded like Gi" Amora chuckled. "She hated when I got so worked up and I use to have panic attacks. She would help me get through them then hit me with her cane afterwards" Amora continued laughing causing everyone else to join in laughter.

"She was deadly with that cane, I caught it a couple time" Dr. Thomas admitted.

"I'm sure you did, she did not discriminate" Amora chuckled as she sipped her water.

"This is probably the wrong time to bring this up but it's so funny and it goes with the stories everyone is telling" Joseline began. "I remember when you, your mother and sister first started attending the church and Ma caught Stephanie hitting you for no reason. I've never seen her move so fast, not even when she was defending me. She went from her porch over to you and Stephanie in under a second and clocked Stephanie so fast with that cane" Joseline reminisced causing Amora to burst into laughter.

"She used to call my mother "the devil" and one time I was standing in front of Gi's house talking to her and my mother was calling for me to come on. So I think my mom said something about if she had to come get me it would be a problem. Child Gi stood up from her little chair and grabbed her cane and pointed it in my mother's direction and was like *'Listen you little devil bitch if you even attempt to hit her in my presence I am going to beat you shitless'*" Amora said mimicking Mrs. Gionna's voice causing everyone to burst into laughter.

"She was something else, as little as she was she didn't have an ounce of fear in her body" Dr. Thomas laughed.

"She would always say fear is a manmade emotion. Whenever I would tell her something I wanted to do she would say okay baby now do it! I would always say I can't Gi I'm scared or I'm not ready and she would always say 'Amora Fear is not something you were born with, it's something you adopted throughout life. You were not created to possess fear; you were created to be bold and courageous. Fear does not exist' and I never understood what she meant until I started my Nonprofit and you know what's crazy" Amora said in deep thought.

"What's that?" Joseline, Sionni and Dr. Thomas all asked.

"After all of these years this is the first time I was actually able to fully understand what she meant by I wasn't practicing what I preached. Here I am telling my students to be fearless and confident and innovative but yet I still live my life in fear and stop myself from reaching my fullest potential. I was living in fear and not realizing how much it effected what I'm put here to do. Fear comes from shame and embarrassment and all of this time Gi has been trying to get me to understand that I have nothing to be embarrassed about! Why didn't I get that sooner?" Amora asked herself.

"Sometimes it takes a person's absence for us to understand what they were place in our life to teach us. She had a tough job that she took pride in and that was to repair everything your mother broke. And with that she had to be patient with you and it took time for you to fully understand many of her lessons. But the good thing is that what she did wasn't in vain because you grasped what she wanted you to" Joseline explained to a crying Amora. "Don't lose what she taught you, carry that throughout the rest of your life and let your light shine Amora stop hiding the world is waiting for you" Joseline added as she embraced an emotional Amora.

It's been three days since Mrs. Gionna passed away and Amora and Joseline with the help of Sionni and Sam have been working overtime to ensure that her home going service is fit for the Queen that she was. Family and friends gathered at Mrs. Gionna's house to offer their love and support. Joseline and Amora were forever grateful for the love they were receiving from everyone.

"Amora the Pastor is on the phone for you. Do you want me to tell him you will call him back when you're finished talking" Sam asked Amora who was in the middle of talking to the florist who is arranging the flower arrangements for the service.

"Um no I'll get it! I'm sorry can you excuse me for a moment?" Amora asked excusing herself and taking the phone from Sam.

"Hello? Pastor how are you?" Amora said as she spoke into the phone.

"The real question is how are you feeling?" He replied.

"I am just taking it day by day" Amora answered honestly.

"Stay in prayer Amora that it where all of your strength will come from." He told her. "I was able to reschedule my preaching engagement so I am able to do the funeral. I just wanted to extend a helping hand if you or Joseline need anything or help with anything please do not hesitate to contact me or my wife we are here to serve during this grieving time" He explained.

"Pastor Carter I appreciate that so much thank you" Amora expressed.

"No problem, God bless you two and I will talk to you soon" He told her before hanging up the phone.

"Everything okay" Sam and Sionni asked as Joseline walked up.

"Yes he just wanted us to know that he is here if we need anything and that he is able to do the Eulogy for the funeral" Amora told them.

"Good Ma loved to hear him preach" Joseline smiled.

"I know I used to send her sermon videos every morning" Amora replied.

"Um Joseline there are two young girls at the door" Mrs. Gionna's neighbor Ms. Rena said as she stood at the door with it open.

"Two young girls for me" Joseline asked confused.

"I'm sorry babies, who are you looking for?" Ms. Rena asked the two girls.

"Ms. Amora" One of them replied.

"Oh I'm sorry, Amora they are looking for you sweat pea" Ms. Rena said moving to the side as Amora walked towards the door.

"That better not be who I think it is" Sam fussed walking behind Amora.

"Hey Ms. Amora girl" Monae greeted as soon as Amora made it to the door. "Before you start tripping because I see the wrinkle forming over top of your eye brow. Relax!" She continued. "We just really wanted to be here for you, we know we shouldn't have followed you here but there was no way we could let you go through this alone" Monae finished with Sierra nodding in agreeance.

"Please tell me someone knows you're here and you didn't just up and leave" Amora pleaded.

"Of course they know well my foster parents knows, I can't speak for Monae" Sierra replied.

"Ms. Amora I'm 18 which means I can now come and go as I please" Monae said defending herself causing Amora to give her the side eye. "But I told them people I was going away, that's all they needed to know anyway they don't be checking for me like that" Monae added.

"Come inside. I want you to call both of your families so I can make sure they are okay with you being here" Amora told them as she moved out the way so they could walk inside.

"Okay" They replied in unison.

"I should have known it wasn't anybody but you two bugga boo's" Sam joked when the girls walked inside of the house.

"Well that wasn't nice Ms. Samantha! What happened to good hospitality?" Monae replied shaking her head causing Amora to laugh.

"Something is wrong with you girl" Amora joked. "Everyone these are two of my students from my program in Atlanta Sierra and Monae. Girls this is everybody! Walk around introduce yourself, watch your mouths and get comfortable. I'm going to assume you planned on staying with me because you're not old enough to book your own room" Amora said to them.

"You assumed right. It was either you or Ms. Samantha! Either way we knew we had a place to stay" Sierra shrugged causing Amora to shake her head then walk away.

"Behave you two! Do not be in here cursing and what not" Sam warned. "Oh Sionni this is Monae and Sierra two of your sister's headache students" Sam introduced them laughing.

"Why yall act like we so out of control or something? Shit I'm well behaved" Monae said causing Sierra to nudge her arm.

"Hey Sionni, it's nice to finally put a face to a name" Sierra said as she hugged Sionni. "Mo she said no cursing! Chill because Ms. Amora might put us out she probably don't have a whole lot of patience right now so chill out Monae because I'm telling you right now if she come over here mad I'm blaming you and I don't care" Sierra told her honestly.

"Snicthes get stitches" Monae whispered to Sierra causing Sionni to laugh as she walked away. The remainder of the day went by without Monae or Sierra giving Amora any problems and she was grateful because she couldn't babysit them and handle everything she was juggling. It was late at night when Joseline was leaving Mrs. Gionna's house and heading home.

"Okay Amora I am going to head on home. I'm beat" Joseline said as she yawned.

"Okay Joseline, I'll see you in the morning!" Amora told her. "You sure you don't want to just sleep here? You know it's more than enough room" Amora offered.

"No I'm good, Ma might think it's funny to mess with me in here and I am in no way ready for that" Joseline answered honestly laughing.

"What about you Si are you staying or going home?" Amora asked her sister.

"I'm going to go home, I don't have any clothes but I'll be over first thing in the morning" Sionni assured Amora.

"Alright have a good night!" Amora told them both as she walked them to the door.

"I really appreciate all you're doing for Ma, I could not have done all this without you" Joseline admitted.

"Don't thank me Gi meant everything to me. And we couldn't have done this without each other. I don't think you've noticed but we've been each other personal support the past couple days." Amora told her.

"I know it's almost like I finally get to feel what it's like having a much younger sister" Joseline laughed.

"Let Gi tell it we are sisters. You couldn't tell her I wasn't her child" Amora laughed.

"You never lied about that! Alright love you see you tomorrow" Joseline said catching Amora off of guard.

"Love you too Jos be careful" Amora replied as she closed the door.

"*What a day*" Amora sighed as she collapsed on the couch. It was the first time Amora had been by herself since leaving the hospital. Glancing around the room her eyes fell on a picture of her and Mrs. Gionna when Amora first came to stay with her.

"Alright baby now you've been here plenty of times so you know where everything is. Make yourself completely at home this is now your home" Mrs. Gionna told Amora as she began to unpack her suitcase.

"I'm happy everything worked out in court. I would have been devastated if I had to go stay with someone else Gi" Amora replied.

"I wouldn't have allowed it. I would have threatened everybody on the list for you to go through Chile they

would have been begging me to take you once I was finished" Mrs. Gionna told Amora seriously.

"Gi you are really crazy" Amora laughed.

"Crazy about my baby! I would go to war with the whole system is they would have separated us" Mrs. Gionna expressed as she walked over and sat next to Amora on the bed.

"Now what?" Amora asked looking around the room.

"Now I teach you how to love yourself so that when I am gone you will know how to search within for the love you need" Mrs. Gionna told her.

"Ms. Amora are you alright?" Sierra asked interrupting Amora's thoughts and sitting next to her on the couch.

"Yes just thinking about Gi that's all" Amora told her honestly.

"She still has you room set up like you were still living here" Sierra stated.

"She said she kept it that way so I would always feel comfortable enough to come back if I couldn't afford my rent" Amora replied laughing causing Sierra to laugh as well.

"She was something else" Sierra admitted.

"You have no idea! Where is Monae?" Amora asked changing the subject.

"Upstairs getting on Ms. Samantha's nerves" Sierra replied laughing.

"Oh lord we better go up there. Sam doesn't have as much patience as me when it comes to you girls" Amora said as she stood up from the couch and headed towards the steps with Sierra right behind her.

"Ms. Samantha you have to understand where I'm coming from. These dudes will drive you crazy if you let them. I damn near lost all my marbles behind this dude because all he wanted to do was lie and I had to turn up on his ass" Monae explained to Sam as Amora and Sierra entered the room.

"Monae what did I tell you about your mouth girl? You cannot curse like that around me! You shouldn't talk like that period, you curse like a sailor" Amora fussed.

"My fault Ms. A pray for me" Monae said causing Amora to laugh. "See you needed me here Ms. Amora I already got you laughing again" Monae boosted.

"I definitely needed that laugh" Amora admitted. "I'm sure Sam wants to get some sleep Monae so come on so I can show you two where you will be sleeping" Amora told them.

"Ms. Amora I mean well when I say this but you are not about to put us off in one of these rooms. Nope we are sleeping in the same room as you. Not in the same bed but on the floor or something" Monae replied seriously causing Amora and Sam to burst into laughter.

"What do you think is going to happen to you if you sleep in a room by yourselves?" Amora asked her.

"I don't know, Mrs. Gionna didn't seem like a very friendly person and she didn't know us. I don't want her to you know start messing with us or something" Monae told Amora.

"If she wanted to bother you girls she would whether you are in the room with me or not" Amora replied laughing. "But if it makes you feel better I'll blow up the air mattress and you can sleep in the room with me" Amora told her causing Monae to smile widely and hug her. "Come on because I'm ready to get in the bed" She added then walked out of the room. Majority of the night Amora tossed and turned unable to get comfortable and find a peaceful sleep. Getting frustrated she got out of bed then walked down stairs to the kitchen to make a cup of tea. Making sure she was quiet she fixed a cup of tea, grabbed Mrs. Gionna's bible and opened it to where Mrs. Gionna's last book mark was placed. When Amora turned to the page a white envelope fell out and onto the table. Grabbing the envelope she noticed that it had her name on it written in Mrs. Gionna hand writing causing Amora to rip it open and read it carefully.

My Sweet Amora,

If you are reading this, it only means that I am finally with the lord. I said finally because I was getting old chile. I know you have a ton of questions and you're filled with many emotions one of which may be anger but don't be my sweet baby. I chose not to allow the doctor's to operate because I already knew I would not make it out alive. I couldn't put you all through the pressure of watching me never come out of what the doctors claimed I would. I accepted my mission in life and completed it with everything in me. I know you feel like I left and abondened you Amora but I promise I didn't. I placed every principle that you adore me for inside of you so you have me everywhere you go. Baby I'm old there is no way my body or brain could have withstood that type of procedure. I already knew my fate and I was okay with it because I don't feel like I'm leaving you, my spirit will forever be with you. You need to talk? Talk to me I promise I'll be right there. You need to see me? I promise I'm showing up. I'm forever with you! Remember the promise you made to me on the phone. Change the world baby! You are special and you have so much to show the world about love and forgiveness and about God! Show the world what he did for you Amora, It was not me it was all in his plan. I love you so very much and celebrate with me because I am happy and at peace.

P.S Do not let Joseline put one of those ugly church hats on me at my funeral. I would like to be very beautiful and elegant.

I'll always be there when you need me the most, but for everything lean on God Amora

Unable to stop the tears from falling from her eyes, Amora dropped the letter then dropped her head on the table letting out a gut wrenching cry. *"I just don't get it"* She cried. "You should have told me, I would have helped you. Why didn't you tell me Gi" She continued to cry loudly. Peeking into the kitchen, Sierra contemplated on whether she should embrace Amora or leave her alone. "God I need you so bad right now! I can't explain this level of hurt I'm feeling. What am I supposed to do without her, she was the only family I had why would you take her from me" Amora cried angrily. Unable to walk away, Sierra grabbed a box of tissues from off of the counter and walked over to Amora handing them to her. Looking up at Sierra with teary eyes, Amora accepted the tissues and began to wipe the snot running from her nose.

"Ms. Amora I'm sorry for invading your personal space but I couldn't sit upstairs and not come down here after hearing your cries. I'm going to hug you because I don't know of any other way to comfort you right now" Sierra expressed before embracing Amora and allowing her to cry on her shoulder. "I don't know much Ms. Amora but I do know your religion and faith in God got you through a lot so turn to him now. I've never seen you do anything other smile so to see you so hurt like this it's making me sad so we are going to cry together because I know this hurt bad" Sierra told Amora as they both hugged each other and cried.

"I'm sorry Sierra, I didn't mean to break down like that" Amora apologized.

"It's okay to cry Ms. Amora you don't have to be strong all the time! You're hurting and it's okay to express that!" Sierra said as she rubbed Amora's back.

"How are you going to use my techniques against me" Amora chuckled and sniffled.

"Sometimes we have to take our own advice" Sierra said shocking Amora. Instead of replying Amora took a sip of her tea and sat there in deep thought. Without another word being said, Sierra and Amora both retreated back upstairs to get some much needed rest. The next morning Amora was awaken by the sound of people talking and laughing under her. Grabbing her phone and checking the time she couldn't believe she had slept majority of the day away. Ignoring the many call and text messages she missed, Amora got out of bed then got dressed so that she could join everyone downstairs. After washing and throwing on a comfortable sweat suit with a pair of sneakers, she braided her hair in two French braids and left the room.

"Ooop Ms. A you are giving me life dressed down like that" Monae complimented dramatically when Amora walked down the steps.

"You're so silly! Did you girls eat already? I'm starving" Amora said while looking around and smiling at all of the people that crowded Mrs. Gionna's living room.

"No, Ms. Samantha tried to make us eat some nasty food Mrs. Gionna's neighbor brought over but I just couldn't" Sierra replied with her face balled up.

"Let me go and check on Joseline then we will go to the mall and grab something to eat afterwards" Amora told them before walking off.

"Sleeping beauty is finally awake" Joesline said as she smiled and embraced Amora.

"Girl I needed that rest" Amora admitted and chuckled. "Do you need my help with anything before I go? I'm going to get some air and take the girls to the mall and to grab something to eat" Amora told her.

"No I'm fine you go and enjoy yourself. Get your mind off of everything here I've got it covered" Joseline assured her.

"Do you need anything?" Amora asked her.

"No I'm good. If I think of something I will just call you. Are you okay though? Sam told me you had a rough night last night" Joseline said pulling Amora to the side.

"I did! But I'm fine now well for now at least" Amora chuckled. "I should be asking you if you're okay! You all worried about me how are you holding up?" Amora asked.

"I'm still standing that's all that matters. You know how me and Ma relationship was, we went years not talking even after she took you in we still weren't on the best of terms and I just feel like a fool for going so long without speaking to my mother when all she was doing was trying to protect me" Joseline expressed.

"Regardless of how tough Gi tried to portray herself to be regarding you and her relationship I know it hurt her just as much as it hurt you. The good thing is that you both came together and was able to make up for time lost before she passed" Amora told her.

"I can see why Ma was so drawn to you" Joseline said as she admired Amora.

"Why you say that?" Amora asked.

"You're beautiful on the inside an out! It's amazing how through all of the ugly things that were done to you in the past you still have this amazing aura about you that's just so inviting and comforting. Even in the midst of hurting and grieving" Joseline expressed.

"Thank you! You have God and your mother to thank for that. Because if it was up to me I surely would have been done with people a very long time" Amora stated.

"And nobody could blame you for that given all you've experienced" Joseline told her.

"Yeah well I'm going to get out of here. I'll see you later" Amora told her before walking away. "You girls ready?" She asked as she walked back into the living room.

"Hell yeah" Monae jumped with excitement.

"Monae" Sam scolded.

"I meant Heck yeah!" She said quickly. "Bare with me Ms. A I'm trying" Monae told her.

"Yeah whatever girl! You're lucky I don't have the energy to tell you about yourself, but we're going to talk" Amora told her as she walked out of the door and got into her car.

"Awe come on Ms. A I'm sorry! You're not going to send me home are you?" Monae pouted. "Is your sister coming with us?" She asked Amora

"Speaking of home, when exactly are your flights scheduled to leave? And no Sionni has to work" Amora said to them.

"Sunday" Monae replied.

"Sunday? How in the hell did the two of you think that you could just skip school for an entire week to fly down here to be with me? I get that you were trying to comfort me and support me but you two should have discussed it with me first! Do your parents know you planned to stay this long?" Amora fussed at them.

"It's spring break Ms. Amora." Sierra spoke calmly. Instead of responding Amora turned on the radio and drove to the mall in deep thought. After shopping for over an hour, Amora, Sam, Sierra and Monae all sat down to eat at Bahama Breeze.

"Hello welcome to Bahama Breeze, my name is Alison and I'll be your waitress this evening. Can I start you off with something to drink?" The waitress asked.

"Can I get a shot of Hennessy and a Patron Margarita with a glass of water on the side" Amora said never taking her eyes off of the menu.

"I'll take a strawberry lemonade" Sierra said ordering next.

"I'll have a patron margarita as well" Sam told the waitress.

"I'll have the same" Monae said causing everyone to look her way. "I'm stressing just like yall, Ms. Amora I figured one for the occasion wouldn't hurt" Monae shrugged.

"She will a strawberry lemonade as well" Amora told the waitress before rolling her eyes at Monae then looking back at her menu.

"Mo you gotta chill" Sierra told her laughing.

"I want to apologize to you girls for snapping earlier. I am a big ball of emotions right now so please bare with me" Amora said to them.

"It's cool Ms. A we didn't take any offense to it. If anything you should have because you were the salty one" Sierra joked.

"I didn't even know what to say that's why I just turned the music up" Amora said laughing as the waitress returned with their drinks.

"Are you guys ready to order?" The waitress asked them.

"Yeah I'll have the jerk chicken pasta and the spinach dip for the table please" Amora said ordering first.

"Can I get the chicken and shrimp Alfredo with a side of broccoli" Sierra ordered next.

"I'll take the jerk chicken with a Caesar salad" Sam told the waitress.

"Ms. Samantha let me find out you on a diet" Monae joked. "I'll take the salmon with a fully loaded bake potato and spinach" Monae finished.

"Okay I'll put your order in and get your food right out" The waitress told them before walking away.

"I can't wait to get my food! I haven't had some alfredo in like two days" Sierra said.

"Si all you eat is Alfredo, you can go without it for two days" Monae told her.

"Is Alfredo your favorite food Sierra?" Amora asked.

"Yes I love alfredo" Sierra emphasized.

"Me too; well I used to especially when I was younger. Gi used to make it for me all the time" Amora said as she began to daydream.

"She was a good cook?" Monae asked.

"Yes! She could cook her little behind off" Amora said smiling with tears forming in her eyes.

"How long was it before you finally moved in with her?" Sierra asked.

"When I woke up in the hospital, Gi never let me out of her sight after that. She refused to let me go back to my mother's house. So I moved in with her then" Amora told them.

"How did your mother take that? What even happened to her?" Monae asked.

"Well the morning I woke up in the hospital and Gi asked me if I remembered what happened she asked me if I could tell her; so I did!" Amora began.

Past

"If it's too much for you to deal with right now, Amora you don't have to tell me just yet! We can wait baby" Gi said to me causing me to shake my head no.

"No Gi I want to tell you because you have to help me! I can't go back to my mother's house" I told her.

168

"Well you weren't going back there anyway. But I need you tell me what happened so that I know how I have to handle the police" She explained.

"After the confrontation between you and my mother we went home and I immediately tried to go to my room to get away from her because I knew she was still mad about what happened between the two of you. But before I could get up the steps she stopped me.

"Amora tell me what you told that old woman and why she felt like she could ever call me out on anything I do to you.' My mother said to me stopping me in my tracks.

"Mom I already told you I didn't tell her anything, she was speaking off of what she has seen you do to me outside of the church multiple times" I told her.

"You're lying!" She screamed then grabbed me by my hair.

"Let me go mom! What is wrong with you?" I screamed trying to break free from her tight grip.

"No I'm sick of you! I'm going to teach you watch!" She threatened then began to punch me in my face and head. I threw my hands up in attempt to block the blows, eventually I balled up in a ball and continued screaming for her to stop. It was as if she was in a daze because she had this scary look in her eyes as she ignored my cries and continued to rain blows all over my body. She eventually got tired of swinging and began to stomp and kick me repeatedly in the head before climbing on top of me.

"I promise when I'm finished with you, you're never going to want to go against me again" She seethed as she gripped my shirt and began to bang me into the floor. Hearing your words in my head *"You're going to have to stand up for yourself Amora. You put an end to the abuse"* I mustered up every bit of strength I had left in me and pushed my mother off of me. She quickly grabbed a hand full of my hair as we switched roles and she was now underneath of me. "Let go of my hair mom" I said to her.

"Oh you think you're tough?" She asked as she stood to her feet, threw me on the steps and began banging my head on the steps. I refused to take any more of the abuse so I kneed my mother right in her vagina causing her to fall over and off of me. I took that opportunity to run straight for the front door, I knew that if I could get to your house I would be safe. "I had enough of you and this abuse. I'm leaving and never coming back, I don't deserve this" I screamed with tears pouring from my eyes as my hand touched the front door.

"You're not going nowhere little girl get back here" My mother yelled as she stood to her feet and ran towards me.

I didn't bother to respond instead I hurriedly turned and opened the door only to run straight into Damien's chest. "Going somewhere beautiful?" He asked as he caught me before I hit the ground.

"No she's not! Bring her little grown ass back in here" My mother told Damien who released his grip on me then pushed me back inside the house.

"What's going on in here?" Damien asked looking between my mother and I.

"She was being disobedient and had to be taught a lesson" My mother said looking at me with fire in her eyes. "Then she thought she was tough and decided she wanted to hit me back" She added.

"Oh no beautiful you can't disrespect your mother!" Damien said to me "Why don't you apologize." He suggested.

"No! I didn't do anything and I'm not sorry for hitting her because she always hits me and beats me up for no reason. Look at my face!!" I screamed then pointed to the knot on my forehead and the blood coming from my nose and mouth.

"Why don't you go upstairs and get cleaned up while I talk to your mother!" Damien told me. Without hesitating I took off up the stairs and away from both of them.

 Running straight to my room, I wasted no time in locking the door behind me. Glancing around my room, I stood there confused; I never left my room amess and here I was looking at all of my things thrown all over the place. *What was she in here looking for?"* I mumbled to myself as I continued to look around the room. Stepping over piles of clothes that's was thrown from my drawers, I lift my mattress up and that's when I noticed that my diary was missing. I began to panic because of everything that was written inside of there. "You've got to be kidding me man, where is my freaking diary?" I screamed angrily. "Give me my diary back!" I demanded as I stormed out of my room and stood at the top of the steps looking down at my mother who was seated on the bottom step.

"I'm not giving you shit!" My mother said to me nonchalantly over her shoulder and in all honesty it pissed me off so bad.

"What you mean? It's not yours, it's mine, and it's my privacy!" I screamed with so much anger that spit flew out of my mouth.

"This is my house; you don't get any privacy in this mother fucker. You want privacy? Get out!" She yelled back at me.

"I'm sick of you! You're evil for no reason, you go to church three times a week you would think that you would be a kind hearted individual but you're not! I don't understand you, what do you get out of treating me the way you do? Does it make you feel good about yourself?" I asked her as I began to slowly walk down the steps. I don't where that boast of courage came from but when I say I fed up I was fed up.

"As a matter of fact, it does! I enjoy seeing you hurt and unable to defend yourself. I enjoy telling you how much I hate you because I really do. I enjoy seeing all the marks and bruises left on that pretty little face of yours after I kick your ass. I enjoy every minute of it" She smiled devilishly as she turned to face me.

"You're sick! You know what I'm not even mad at you, disappointed yes but mad no! You need help, how can you say you enjoy doing all that stuff to a child you gave birth to? And since we are talking about sick people, Damien you're sick for what you did to me! You're a grown man with a bunch of woman running after you yet you just had to rape me. IM A CHILD!!!!" I screamed at the top of my lungs with tears pouring down my face.

"Watch your mouth beautiful, talking to me like that will result in you being punished" Damien said as he stared at me.

"You think you so tough huh? Bring your little ass all the way down the steps with all that mouth" Stephanie challenged

"I'm not afraid of you anymore; there is nothing you can do to me that you haven't already done. What's next? You're going to kill me Stephanie?" I smirked devilishly back at her.

"That can be arranged" She replied before pulling my diary from behind her back and tossing it at me. "You think it's cool to write all that shit down? What if somebody else got they hands on it other than me or Damien? Then what?" She asked me angrily.

"Then the both of you would be held accountable for everything you've done to me. If you didn't do those things, I wouldn't have anything bad to write about and we wouldn't have this problem now would we?" I told her bending down to pick my diary up off of the steps. Taking that opportunity to make her move, my mother ran up the few steps that separated the two us and yanked me towards her then threw me on the couch. Holding my hands together and securing my legs underneath her so I couldn't move nor fight back, my mother turned around and gave Damien and nod of approval for him to make his way over to us.

"You see beautiful all this time you had me fooled, I thought you were this innocent shy girl who didn't say or do much but you're the complete opposite" Damien said as he began to unbuckle his pants. "There are consequences for every action and you must be punished for how you carried on in here today" He told me.

"My innocence was snatched from me or have you forgotten Damien?" I said with tears in my eyes. Watching Damien unbuckle his pants I feared the worst was about to happen to me all over again. "Please don't do this again" I begged and began to cry uncontrollably.

"When my women disrespect me they must make it up by making me feel good and you beautiful are no exception" Damien said as he massaged his penis and positioned himself over top of me with my mother still holding me down. "Open wide baby, I want to see what your mouth feels like" He said to me before forcing his penis inside of my mouth and then moaning. Unable to get him off of me any other way because I was confined, I did the only thing I felt like I could do at that point which was to bite down on Damien's penis. So that's what I did, I bit down so hard hoping I drew blood in the process.

"AHHHHHHH! You stupid little bitch! Let my dick go!" Damien screamed in pain.

"Amora open your mouth!" My mother yelled frantically but I was not budging.

"Open your mouth! AHHHHHH!!!" Damien continued to scream. Realizing that I was not going to let up, he did the only thing he knew he could which was to knock me out. Damien punched me so hard that my mouth flew open and I was knocked out cold.

"Gi I don't remember anything after that! How did I end up here, how did you even find me?" I said to Mrs. Gionna as I struggled to remember what happened next.

"You butt dialed me, I heard the entire thing and jumped straight in my car!" She told me. "I'm proud of you for standing up for yourself. You should have seen your mothers face when me and my little boo showed up at that front door with my gun pointed right at her. She talked her shit and I kept my gun pointed right at her. I looked behind her and that damn Pastor was passed out with blood coming from his private area and child when I saw that I panicked. I cold clocked your mom with my gun, and rushed inside and saw you passed out on the couch with a face full of blood and lumps on your head. I had my friend pick you up and we brought you here!" Mrs. Gionna told me.

"Sorry to interrupt but I just came to check your vitals and give you an update of your test results" The doctor said as he walked inside of my hospital room. "I'm sure you don't remember what happened to you because you were in pretty bad shape when you got here but you're healing beautifully. You did suffer a concussion so you will experience headaches here and there but don't worry whenever you feel one just let the nurse know and she will give you medicine for it. You have a broken nose which is why it's bandaged up right now but that will heal fine. We tested you for STD's just as a precaution because we weren't exactly sure of everything that has happened to you. We also ran a pregnancy test which came back positive. Amora you are six weeks pregnant" The doctor told me shocking the hell out me and Mrs. Gionna. My mouth flew open and Mrs. Gionna dramatically fell to the floor.

Present

"Here you go ladies" The waitress said as she began to place their food on the table.

"Ms. A you did exactly what I would have done. I would have bit that man penis completely off then I would have spit it at my mother" Monae said angrily ignoring the fact that the waitress was standing there.

"Omg Monae what the hell" Sam replied choking on her drink.

"Wait Ms. A you had a baby?" Sierra asked shockingly.

"Thank you so much" Amora said to the waitress before addressing Sierra. "To answer your question no I do not have a baby, however I was pregnant" Amora told her.

"You got an abortion or you miscarried?" Monae asked.

"Oh my god Mo why does that matter? She doesn't have a baby that's all we need to know" Sierra snapped.

"No it's okay Sierra! No need to get upset, I'm not offended." Amora assured Sierra. "I got an abortion Monae! There was no way in hell I could carry that baby" Amora told her as she stuffed her mouth full of the pasta she ordered.

"How was that for you?" Sierra asked.

"Horrible but Gi always knew how to turn a negative situation and make it comical" Amora chuckled as she sipped her margarita.

"What did she do?" Monae asked excitingly.

"You like Gi a little too much Monae" Amora joked.

"From one crazy to another we appreciate the craziness of our peers" Monae said causing everyone to burst into laughter.

"I really wish the two of you could have met, she would have loved you" Amora said laughing. "Once Gi decided that she wanted to faint; every doctor and nurse that was on the floor rushed into my hospital room" Amora began picking up where she left off.

Past

"Gi did you have to fall to the ground like that? You had all the doctors and nurses panicking" I fussed at her once I saw her eyes peak open.

"I wasn't the hell joking, why you let them leave me on the floor like that" She asked as she popped me in my shoulder.

"I just find it really ironic how you weren't joking but your eyes sure did pop open the moment they left the room. And I didn't let them leave you on the floor crazy lady how you think you woke up in the bed next to me? I didn't pick you up Gi" I laughed at her.

"How are you feeling baby? You know after hearing what the doctor said. What's going on in that head of yours?" She asked me switching the topic.

"Gi to be honest with you I couldn't even tell you if I tried. I'm so confused, I'm hurt, I'm angry, I'm disgusted. It's almost like I'm just destined for bad things to happen to me because that's all that ever happens to me. What am I supposed to do with a baby? You know my mother is not going to let that fly, I'm surprised she hasn't come bursting through those doors causing a scene yet" I said as tears threatened to fall from my eyes.

"You know I can't let you go back to that house Amora it's completely out of the question. I can't continue to sit around and do nothing. It's killing me every time you are there because I worry what is going to happen to you next. I need you to let me help you" She reasoned with me.

"I know Gi, I'm just so scared I don't want anything to happen to you and I don't want to make things worse than they already are" I said as I wiped my eyes with the tissues I was holding. "Keeping this baby is not something I can imagine right now Gi, I'm only 15 what am I going to do with a baby? A baby that came from me being raped, I can't keep it!" I continued with my face covered in tears.

"Amora listen to me nobody is going to fault you for making that decision. That is something you have to live with for the rest of your life not anyone else so who the hell cares what anyone has to say. Only you know what is too much for you and baby girl if ending this pregnancy is something you feel you have to do I support you one hundred percent" She told me sincerely.

"Mrs. Gionna I'm glad you finally decided to wake up! You gave us quite a scare beautiful" The walking back inside the room.

"You should have gave me mouth to mouth then maybe I would have woken up sooner" She flirted causing me to spit out the water I was sipping on.

"Gi you didn't just say that" I said to her in between laughs.

"Mrs. Gionna you are something else! He told her smirking. I came in here to check on you ladies, your reaction to the news I shared wasn't exactly good so I wanted to make sure you two were alright before I ended my shift" He added.

"I'm only 15 what am I supposed to do with a baby? I can barely take care of myself Gi" I spoke and shook my head.

"How would we go about getting it taken care of doctor, she made her decision so it is something the hospital can take care of or do I have to take her to a clinic?" Mrs. Gionna asked him.

"Are you her guardian?" He asked Mrs. Gionna.

"Yes! She lied with a straight face causing me to side eye her.

"Well because Amora's pregnancy is not threatening her life or the health of the baby, the hospital will not perform the abortion so you would have to schedule her appointment at an abortion clinic. I can recommend you to some if you like" He told her.

"How much longer do I have to stay here?" I asked him.

"Yeah doctor we are ready to go" Mrs. Gionna cosigned.

"Mrs. Gionna you're free to go whenever you are ready you are not the one that's admitted" He joked but she didn't find anything funny and I think he caught her drift by the way she was looked at him. "I'm just joking beautiful don't kill me" He cleared up quickly then winked.

"You better stop while you're a head boy because an experienced woman like me will have you hooked" She told him as she reached for her cane then got out of the bed we both were laying in.

"Gi can you stop flirting with him so he can answer my questions" I asked her shaking my head.

"That's not me, he starting with me! I'll be quiet from now on. I have to use the restroom" She said to me before walking inside of the bathroom and closing the door behind her.

"You have to excuse her doctor she just a little crazy" I said to the doctor once Mrs. Gionna was gone.

"She is a piece of work" He laughed "We are going to keep you for one more night and you are free to go in the morning beautiful" He told me shaking his head.

"Amora is fine, please don't call me beautiful" I said correcting him.

"I didn't mean to offend you! But my shift is over so the nurses will be in to check on you throughout the day to ensure that you are comfortable and you don't need anything" He told me.

"Okay thank you" I replied.

"I should sue this entire hospital how did yall have my daughter admitted here for over a week and no one called to notify her mother until now" My mother's loud mouth cursed at the nurses outside of my hospital room.

"Excuse me for a second, I have to see what's going on out there" The doctor said as he rushed out the door the moment Mrs. Gionna came rushing out of the bathroom.

"Gi I told you she would show up" I said frantically before my mother came bursting through the door.

"Amora get the fuck out of that bed and let's go" She demanded.

"Over my dead body" Mrs. Gionna spoke with venom as she stood in front of me to block my mother from getting any closer.

"Enough is enough Gionna! I am seconds away from getting you arrested. Amora is not your concern; she is my daughter and what goes on in my house in none of your concern. Now Amora get up and let's go!" My mother attempting to push her way passed Mrs. Gionna.

"You can't possibly think that is going to fly with me Stephanie" She said sticking her cane out to block my mother's path. "Since you are so very hard of hearing let me explain to you again how this is going to go. You are going to turn around and walk out of here, you aren't going to call the police because come on you and I both know who has a better chance of walking out of there free once everything is revealed. Now leave this baby alone and go get help Stephanie because something is the hell wrong with you but you will not hurt her anymore and I mean that" Mrs. Gionna said to my mother sternly.

"Are you sure you want to play this game with me Gionna?" My mother asked her.

"No the real question is, are you sure you're ready for what I have for you if come near her again!" Mrs. Gionna threatened. "That little knock I gave you upside your head don't compare to what else I have tucked for you!" She added.

"Yeah we'll see" My mother said before storming out the room and slamming the door shut.

"Now what Gi" I asked as I turned to look at her with tears streaming down my face.

"I'll protect you forever and ever" She told me as she hugged me.

"You promise?" I asked lifting my head up to look at her.

"I promise" She replied before kissing my head then pulling me close to her. Gi remained true to her word and kept her promise to me, she meant it when she said she was not letting me go back into that house and she didn't.

The next morning I was released from the hospital and Gi took me straight to the abortion clinic. The experience was something I never want to experience again in my life but it was necessary. There was no way that I could have that baby. I was left recovering from the procedure for a couple days and Gi waited on me hand and foot never once leaving my side. My mother had not once tried to show up again which was strange to me but it was only confirmation for me that she had something up her sleeve. A week after I had my abortion I told Gi that I was ready to go to the police so that if and when my mother decided to pop up Gi already had the needed paperwork, to keep my mother from taking me back well at least at the moment anyway.

"Alright Amora let me do the talking! And if for any reason they need to know everything don't be afraid. I don't care what happens I will not allow you to go anywhere with your mother so it's okay to tell the police the truth. Okay?" Mrs. Gionna said to me as we stood in front of the police station.

"Okay Gi" I replied as we walked through the doors.

"Hello how are you? I am here to file a restraining order against two people" Mrs. Gionna told the officer sitting behind the desk.

"Are you filing for yourself or for someone else" The officer asked as another officer walked a crying woman with her head down out of his office.

"Don't worry Ms. Smith we will do everything in our power to find your daughter" The officer said comforting her causing me to look up.

"Mom?" I said causing her to stop crying and look up.

"Amora Omg Amora thank god you are okay! Where have you been? I thought something happened to you! Oh my God let's go home" She said in one breathe pulling me from the seat I was sitting in.

"Stephanie you know damn well she was not missing just like you know damn well she isn't going anywhere with you" Mrs. Gionna said walking over to both of us.

"Excuse me Ma'am who are you? And how did you end up with her. Her mother reported her missing almost a week ago" The officer said intervening.

"My name is Mrs. Gionna Boyd, what's your name suga?" Mrs. Gionna asked him as he held his hand out.

"I'm Lutinent Daniels. Can someone please explain to me what's going on? How did you end up with the young girl? And how did you report her missing if the three of you clearly know each other?" He asked everyone.

"Stephanie would you like to do the honors or should I? Mrs. Gionna smirked with her arms folded.

"How about you tell me what's going on beautiful" The officer said causing me to cringe.

"My name is Amora officer please don't call me beautiful" I said correcting him. "What exactly do you want me to tell you?" I asked him as I hesitantly looked at my mother who was threatening me with her eyes.

"It's okay Amora, she can't hurt you anymore. Stephanie that look isn't doing anything but making you look cross eyed! All of that intimidation crap ends today" Mrs. Gionna said causing me to look at her and smile.

"How about you tell me where you've been the past week" Luetinent Daniels said to me ignoring the back and forth Gi and my mother were doing.

"I've actually been away from my mother for over two weeks. For the first week I was in the hospital and for the past week I've been at Mrs. Gionna's house" I told him truthfully.

"Why were you in the hospital for a week?" He asked me.

"I was attacked and had to recover from the bruising" I told him.

"Attacked by who?" He asked.

"Umm" I said hesitant because once the words left my mouth there was no turning back.

"It's okay baby" Mrs. Gionna assured me as she walked closer to me.

"Umm I was attacked by my mother and her boyfriend Damien" I told him.

"Attacked how?" He asked as he cut his eyes as my mother who began to fidget.

"Which time" Mrs. Gionna intervened with her hand on her hip.

"Amora let's go! Officer it's clear she is afraid and Mrs. Gionna must have threatened her some kind of way because she is making up lies" My mother said with tears in her eyes.

"You will not be going anywhere Ms. Smith! As a matter fact none of you will until I get to the bottom of what's going on" He told my mother. "Johnson I need you to take Mrs. Gionna and Ms. Smith and put them in separate rooms" Lutinent Daniels instructed.

186

"Absolutely not officer, she is a minor an adult has to be present while she is being questioned by you" Stephanie said confidently.

"That's half true Ms. Smith, however only because I want to get to the bottom of this peacefully I am going to obliged. Amora who would you feel more comfortable talking in front of?" He asked me.

"Mrs. Gionna" I told him quickly.

"Johnson put Ms. Smith is room 2 and make sure she is comfortable. No phone calls" He instructed. "Mrs. Gionna and Amora you two can follow me" He said as he lead us to a questioning room.

"Officer you just try to get in contact with the boyfriend and get his ass down here since we're getting ready to put everything on the table. His ass plays a huge part in all of this" Mrs. Gionna wasted no time saying.

"What's the boyfriend name?' He asked her.

"Damien West" I said speaking up.

"How about you tell me what Damien did and I will dictate whether I need to bring him in for questioning or not" He told me.

"He raped me" I yelled louder than expected with tears streaming down my face. Before responding he looked to Gi who had pulled out a stack of papers and handed them to him. Lutient Daniels looked over the papers then looked between Mrs. Gionna and I before walking out then returning almost an hour later.

"Amora this is Ms. Lena Dowell with child protective services. I need you to explain to her as well as me everything that has transpired between you, your mother and her boyfriend." Lutinent Daniels said to me.

"Child protective services?" I asked confused.

"Lutinent Daniels and I'm sorry what's your name suga?" Mrs. Gionna said extending her hand to the woman.

"Lena.. Lena Dowell" She said shaking Mrs. Gionna's hand smiling.

"Nice to meet you sweet pea" Mrs. Gionna smiled. "Like I was saying Lutinent Daniel and Ms. Dowell with all due respect but you two have sadly mistaken if either of you think Amora is not leaving this building with me. I brought her here so that we could do this the right way because I'm sure you both know how ugly situations like this can get. Now what we are going to do is, Amora is going to tell you everything that has happened enough for you all to build a case not only against Stephanie but also against Damien then I am going to adopt Amora. I'm more than qualified, this child has been through enough I will not allow you to ship her through group home and foster homes where she can possible be placed under the care of people like those she is trying to get away from. No need to reply let's just all agree to do what's in best interest for this innocent child who I will not allow to be hurt anymore" Mrs. Gionna told them confidently.

"Okay" They both replied respectfully shocking me completely. I for sure thought everything was about to go bad once child protective services were involved.

"Amora!" Mrs. Gionna said walking over to me. "Everything is going to be okay! You can tell them everything and do not be afraid. They are not going to take you away from me and I intend to keep my promise. You will be leaving with me once all of this is over" She told me then looked at both Ms. Dowell and Lutinent Daniels who nodded their heads in agreeance. Two hours later after I finished telling them both everything that happened; Mrs. Gionna wasn't the only angry adult in the room.

Present

"I'm sorry to interrupt ladies, but I just came to check on you. Did you need anything else?" The waitress said interrupting Amora's story telling.

"Oh no you're fine. Can I have another margarita and a box for my food please" Amora told her. "Did you girls want anything else?" She asked the table.

"No I'm good" Monae and Sam replied

"I'll take a brownie Sunday with extra brownie and water with lemon" Sierra told the waitress.

"First of all Ms. A, who did Mrs. Gionna think she was? She played no games when it came to you" Monae said as soon as the waitress walked away.

"Monae you would have thought they worked for her. And when I say she kept every promise she kept her word on everything she ever said to me" Amora replied.

"So what happened after you told Officer Daniels and the child protective services lady what happened?" Sierra asked.

"All hell broke loose" Amora chuckled shaking her head.

"Ouuuu Ms. A tell me I know Mrs. Gi was in there causing wreck" Monae laughed amped up.

Past

"Mrs. Gionna, uhh Lutinent Daniels stated that you provided him with some paperwork to support everything that was just told to us" Ms. Dowell said.

"Of course" Mrs. Gionna said handing her another stack of papers she removed from her purse.

"Gi how many copies did you make?" I whispered to her.

"A lot" She told me. "I have a copy for every person that is going to help put them two sick individuals away" She said patting her purse.

"What about witnesses? Can anyone else verify these incidents?" Ms. Dowell asked.

"You have written statements from every nurse and doctor that looked after Amora. You have the results from the rape kit they performed on her the night she was brought into the hospital. You have a written statement from someone who is very close to Damien who is willing to testify in court if need be. Ms. Dowell when we came here I insured that we were prepared. Listed on the back of the stack of papers in contact information for each person willing to testify against both Stephanie and Damien based off of what they personally witnessed them do to Amora." Mrs. Gionna stated.

"I guess the only thing left to ask is, are you sure you want to press charges. Once you go there it's no coming back" Ms. Dowell said.

"Baby even with all of this information sitting in front you, you still feel the need to ask unnecessary questions" Mrs. Gionna said to Ms. Dowell.

"I was just ensuring that you two knew what this entire procedure Intel's" Ms. Dowell said to Mrs. Gionna.

"Lutinent is this enough information for you to charge the two of them and build a case?" Mrs. Gionna asked ignoring Ms. Dowell.

"Absolutely" He replied standing to his feet. "You two hang tight, the two of you will be here for a while. Can I get you anything to make you more comfortable?" He asked us.

"Water is fine" Mrs. Gionna said to him. Lutineint Daniels left the room and did not return for another two hours.

"Umm this case has gotten really interesting" Lutinent Daniels said as he returned to the room we were sitting in.

"How so" Mrs. Gionna asked him.

"Amora do you know of someone by the name of Sunny Tillard?" Lutinent Daniels asked as he sat across from me holding a folder with a stack of papers inside.

"That's my aunt on my father's side. Why?" I asked him.

"She is here" Lutinent Daniel's replied.

"Here for what? I thought I made myself clear when I said Amora is not leaving with anyone but me" Mrs. Gionna said getting up from the chair she was seated in.

"Relax Mrs. Gionna, I heard you loud and clear!" He told her. "Apparently Ms. Tillard came in today unaware that the four of you were already here. She came to report an incident and conversation she had with a co-worker which ties into the story you told us already Amora" He continued.

"I'm sorry what?" I asked him confused.

"Are you familiar with a man by the name of Timothy Carter?" He asked me.

"No that name doesn't ring a bell" I told him.

"Who is he? And what does him and Sunny have to do with this?" Mrs. Gionna asked.

"Timothy Carter apparently told Sunny Tillard that he prayed over Amora in church. He claims that after the situation at church he and Damien had a conversation which led him to believe that there has been some foul play between Amora and Damien. Accordingly to Sunny, she and Timothy Carter work together and he shared with her the conversation he and Damien had. Eventually he revealed a name to the young girl and Sunny discovered that the young girl he was telling her about was Amora. So she brought the information here stating that after several attempts she could not get ahold of Amora nor Stephanie" Lutient Daniels explained to us.

"Would you look at that?" Mrs. Gionna said in disbelief.

"Pastor Carter" I said just above a whisper.

"I'm sorry, what did you say Amora?' Lutinent Daniels asked.

"I know him, but I know him as Pastor Carter. What he said is true! He called me out in church and told my mother to protect me because someone was preying on me" I told him as I thought back to that day.

"So what they are saying is true?" He asked me.

"Yes" I replied.

"I've never had a case be handed to me with all of the evident included" Lutinent Daniels said as stopped the recording.

"One more thing but I'm not sure if we should discuss this is private Mrs. Gionna" He stated looking at her.

"Why what's the matter?" She asked him.

"The witness listed on the back Joseline Boyd, is here as well" He began.

"Okay and?" Mrs. Gionna said to him.

"She has handed over evidence linking Damien to three other young girl's alleged rapes" He told her.

"Three" Mrs. Gionna and I both said in unison.

"By your reaction I assume you didn't know about the others" He said looking between the two of us. "I thought this is why you told me to contact her. She made my job easy because she was already here when I was walking Pastor Carter out" He finished.

"No I told you to contact her about another young girl that she felt may have been a victim of Damien's. I had no clue that there were actually three other girls" Mrs. Gionna replied confused.

"She was unaware that it was this many too. As she was gathering information on the one she stumbled across the information about the other two. Umm Mrs. Gionna I've to be honest with you, although Stephanie plays a huge part in Amora's case and she will more than likely serve time. However her punishment will not be as harsh as Damien's especially given all of these with the testimonies of several people who have seen Damien repeatedly beat on

Stephanie. I am telling you this because she may be defended as a victim of domestic abuse." Lutinent Daniels broke down to us.

Present

"Domestic abuse! How in the hell did your mother manage to pull that off?" Monae asked angrily.

"According to a witness that they never disclosed the identity of, who brought forth crucial evidence that supported the domestic abuse plea" Amora replied to her.

"Were you mad?" Sierra asked.

"No because I never doubted that he didn't abuse my mother in some way. I've never seen the physical abuse but emotionally and verbally yes, I've witnessed that a few times. I was never mad at my mother I was hurt and needing love that she couldn't give me for whatever reason" Amora told them.

"So you didn't want her to go to jail?" Monae asked.

"No I wanted her to get help and until she did I wanted to be far away from her as possible. I didn't want to be mistreated anymore that's all" Amora explained.

"Ms. Amora you are just too damn nice. I would have told the judge to throw both of them under the jail" Monae said jokingly.

"Damien yes, but my mother no she just needed healing of some sort" Amora replied.

"What kind of healing?" Sierra asked.

"Emotional maybe mental; I don't know I just know she needed something and jail wasn't it. My mother was scared from something" Amora expressed as her phone began to ring.

"Hello?" She spoke into the phone.

"Hey just was checking on you guys! I am about to head home, everybody left for the night. And I'm happy as hell, everyone in my face all day long was so overwhelming" Joseline replied on the other end of the phone.

"Girl tell me about it, but okay we are good. We went shopping and to Bahama Breeze which we are currently still at. We were talking and lost track of time" Amora expressed.

"Okay that's fine. I was just checking in. Are you feeling better?" She asked Amora.

"A little bit, how about you? Have you even gotten a chance to sit down and deal with this?" Amora asked her.

"I'm dealing with it, it will hit me the moment I stop moving consistently I'm sure. But for now I am maintaining. I'm going to lock up, I won't be over until later on in the evening Thursday. I have to drive to go get my mother's eldest sister from Virginia" Joseline told Amora.

"Gi had an older sister?" Amora asked shocked,

"Yes, they haven't spoken in over 35 years, but she decided she wants to come pay her respects" Joseline explained.

"Wow! 35years? That's a long time to go without speaking to your sister" Amora admitted.

"You know how stubborn Ma was, you had one time to give her your ass to kiss and she was done with you. She didn't care who you were" Joseline said chuckling.

"Yes I know" Amora replied laughing.

"Well I'm going to let you go. I'll see you tomorrow and you girls enjoy the rest of your night out! She loved you Amora" Joseline said to Amora.

"I know Jos. You should know she loved you too she never stopped loving or talking about you" Amora told her.

"I know because I know my mama." Joseline smiled into the phone before hanging up.

"Ms. Amora I know you are not about to tell us that we have to finish the story at another time" Monae complained the moment Amora got off of the phone.

"Yes but only until later tonight. The house is empty so we will continue our girl's day and have a girl's night" Amora told them as she took out her card so that she could pay the bill.

"Let me pay bestie" Sam said taking the check from Amora and sliding her card in it instead.

"You didn't have to do that Sam" Amora told her.

"I know! But I wanted to so I did" Sam replied.

"Oh no Ms. Samantha, I hope you didn't just get smart with Ms. A.. Ms., A I know you not gonna take that" Monae instigated.

"What you mean? Take what?" Amora asked confused.

"You're her boss. So shouldn't you be the one able to talk to her anyway you want and not the other way around?" Monae replied.

"Have you ever heard me talk down to Sam?" Amora asked her.

"No" She replied.

"Okay so what makes today any different? I know Sam's personality and not only that, we are best friends who have a lot of respect for one another. If I would have took offense to what she said I wouldn't have addressed it in front you girls that would have been a conversation for Sam and I later. I always pay so if anything I'm appreciative that she took the check. Everything is not meant for you to take offense to and when you become a boss you will realize that your team deserves the same level of respect you get. You always should treat others the way you want to be treated regardless of their position" Amora explained.

"I never thought about it like that" Sierra intervened admiring Amora.

"If you want to be successful in entrepreneurship you have to understand that it takes a team for a successful business to run. Just because I am the CEO doesn't mean that my team doesn't deserve the same treatment as me. They help make sure United Inc. is ran probably just like I do" Amora expressed.

"You learn something new every day" Monae said as Amora's phone began to ring again.

"Hello" Amora answered.

"Hey where are you?" Sionni asked.

"Getting ready to leave Bahama Breeze" Amora told her. "Where are you?" She asked Sionni.

"Sitting outside of Mrs. Gi's house; I thought yall would have been back by now" Sionni said to her.

"We got caught up talking. But we are leaving now! Are you going to wait or do you want me to call you when we get back?" Amora asked her.

"I'll wait for you but that don't mean go make other stops Amora. Come straight here because I'm really tired and I want to cuddle and go to sleep" Sionni whinned.

"Si I am not cuddling with you tonight. We are going to sit up all night and have girl talk" Amora told her.

"Yes we are Amora, I don't care what you have to do. You have to eventually go to sleep so when you do we are going to cuddle! Just like old times" Sionni said causing Amora to laugh.

"You're a pain in butt Si" Amora chuckled.

"I love you too. See you in a second" Sionna told her before hanging up.

"Is your sister coming over Ms. A?" Monae asked.

"Yeah she is waiting outside of Gi's house so we have to get going" Amora told them as she stood up from the table.

"Ms. Amora I love that you love God and all of that, but can we please listen to some other music. I heard enough gospel music to last me the rest of the year" Monae said causing everyone to laugh at her.

"What are you going to do with her?" Sam asked laughing.

"I have no clue, she is a piece of work" Amora replied shaking her head as they got inside of the car and pulled off heading back to Mrs. Gionna's house.

"It's about time" Sionni fussed as soon as Amora stepped out of the car.

"Girl bye, I just talked to you twenty minutes ago" Amora told her waving her off.

"Hey Sionni, I was asking about you all day" Monae said giving her a hug.

"I just bet with your crazy self" Sionni replied laughing.

"Why does everybody keep calling me crazy? I'm just very outspoken" Monae said coming to her own defense.

"Yeah outspoken and crazy" Sierra joked as they all walked in the house and made themselves comfortable.

"There is nothing wrong with me being crazy as long as I know when to turn it down right Ms. Amora?" Monae asked.

"Girl I never told you that! But there is nothing wrong with it as long as you are using your crazy to bring people laughter instead of harm" Amora explained to her.

"I make you laugh don't I?" Monae asked.

"Yes a lot actually" Amora admitted.

"Maybe that's my purpose. To bring people laughter when they are down" Monae said thinking out loud causing Amora to smile before turning her attention back to her phone.

"Amora I thought yall were having girl talk? Get to talking so we can go to sleep. You're not slick, I feel like you just said that because you don't want to cuddle with me tonight" Sionni told her causing everyone to laugh.

"Sionni how old are you, still wanting to cuddle with your sister" Sierra teased.

"17" Sionni answered unashamed.

"Oh girl we are around the same age" Monae said to her.

"Sionni is a big ole baby. My big ole baby. She's always been like that. Right up under me" Amora said smiling at her sister.

"Sionni can I ask you a personal question?" Sierra asked.

"Sure" Sionni replied.

"How did it make you feel as a sister, to watch your mother abuse your sister?" Sierra asked her.

"I fortunately only witnessed the abuse a few times well the physical abuse. But to hear the way my mother use to talk to Amora hurt my feelings so much but there was nothing I could do. Besides love on Amora every chance I got" Sionni replied.

"Is that why you're so affectionate with her? Since we were introduced yesterday I've seen you hug her a million times. Or sit on her lap when she is sitting down. Or like today keep asking to cuddle with her" Sierra asked as she chuckled.

"Yup! I love my sister and I am not afraid or ashamed to love on her. It's always been that way. I admire her so much" Sionni admitted.

"Can I ask why?" Sierra asked.

"Who else do you know that has such an abusive past but yet is so loving and nurturing? Many people who experience the level of hurt Amora has, they are angry, bitter and have so many excuses to defend their messed up ways. Not my sister! She is so loving, she doesn't judge you and she genuinely care about the betterment of others. You girls are lucky to have a mentor like her, I'm lucky enough to call such a beautiful soul my sister" Sionni beamed with admiration.

"Awe thanks Si. I love you too little girl" Amora smiled.

"Yall are too cute" Monae teased. "So Ms. A wassup with the rest of that story?" She added.

"You didn't finish telling them everything?" Sionni asked

"Almost! I stopped at the part where mommy and Damien were at the police station" Amora told Sionni. "Well after Lutinient Daniels explained that my mother would more than likely get off easier than Damien, Gi wasn't too happy about it" Amora began..

Past

"I know you're playing a joke on me" Mrs. Gionna said with her hand on her hip.

"I wish I was Mrs. Gionna but I've been working in this field for over two decades and I'm almost certain that's the route the defense is going to take so you should be prepared for that" He explained to us.

"Can we go now? Do you need Amora for anything else?" Mrs. Gionna asked.

"Mike Smith, Amora's father we tried to contact him but he is away on vacation. He said he would give me a call once he returned to the states" Lutinent told us.

"I'm sure he will. Is that all Lutinient? I'm sure baby girl is starving and sick of all this craziness going on in here. If you have any further question feel free to give me a call" Mrs. Gionna told him as we prepared to leave.

"I will be in contact one day next week with a court date for the preliminary hearing. Also Ms. Dowell is going to schedule a home visit with you to tell you what you have to do to become the legal guardian of Amora" Lutinient broke down to Mrs. Gionna.

"Okay suga, you have a good one" She told him as we prepared to leave. As we were walking down the long hall of rooms I stopped once we reached the room Damien was seated in hand cuffed to the table and looked through the glass window. Almost as if he knew I was standing there looking at him, he smirked, smiled then turned his head. "Don't worry baby girl that sick bastard is going to get everything he deserves. I've got some friends on the inside waiting for his nasty ass to walk through those metal doors" Mrs. Gionna whispered to me.

"Gi what? What friends do you have in jail?" I asked her laughing.

"You'll see" She said and zipped her lips.

Present

"So how much time did they end up giving your mom?" Monae asked breaking Amora from the story.

"My mother was sentenced to 12 years for child abuse, rape and child neglect" Amora told her.

"And what about that nasty Pastor?" Sierra asked.

"He was sentenced to 45 years in prison. He was charged with the rape of myself as well as three other girls. He was charged with two counts of aggravated assault and a gang of other charges" Amora replied.

"45 years? That man should've gotten the death penalty. He is a sick individual" Sierra screamed.

"Did Mrs. Gionna really have people on the inside?" Monae asked.

"Girl yes, she was not joking. At the first court date, Damien couldn't even attend because he was hospitalized and confined to a hospital bed. So he was there via video and those guys really did a number on him. Gi didn't make it any better because as soon as Damien was shown on the screen she burst out laughing" Amora told them shaking her head.

"I know that's right Mrs. Gionna because I would have done the same thing. He deserved that" Monae said clapping.

"Nobody deserves to be harmed Monae" Amora told her.

"What you mean? He raped you and preyed on you as well as other young girls. That man deserved every bit of that ass whooping" Monae defended.

"That wasn't for Gi, nor those guys to decide. Not even you! I would be lying to you if I said a part of me wasn't happy he got his butt kicked but the bigger part of me knew that two wrongs didn't make a right." Amora replied.

"Two wrong don't make a right but two negatives sure do make a positive. I still say that sorry excuse for a pastor deserved more for what he did" Sionni said agreeing with Monae causing Amora to look her way. "Sis I know what you are about to say but sometimes God lets people off easy that deserve to be punished" She added.

"That's not true, we don't know what else God has planned for Damien but it's my job to trust him and believe that whatever he has planned for him is far more better than anything all of us combined can think of" Amora told them.

"How was the entire court process?" Sierra asked.

"Long and draining! I was so happy when both my mother and Damien were sentenced and Mrs. Gionna was granted custody of me. I was finally done with that chapter of my life" Amora said full of relief.

"I know that must have felt good for you" Monae said to her.

"Yes and No. Yes because I was away from my mother as well as Damien. No because I was separated from my sister. Luckily Gi actually liked my aunt Sunny and she loved Sionni so we were able to remain close" Amora expressed.

"My little cry baby self, use to really be upset if we had to skip a weekend together. I hated living separately from my sister but I cared more about her happiness and safety so I dealt with it and got on Mrs. Gionna's nerves in the process" Sionni said laughing.

"She is not lying. Sionni used to call me a hundred times a day once she was home from school. She even used to want to fall asleep on the phone. Gi used to fuss at us all the time for tying up her phone line" Amora said laughing.

"Sionni you're worse than me! I'm clingy too but not that bad" Sierra told her laughing.

"I can't help it" Sionni shrugged while laughing. "I don't care though as long as Amora don't have a problem with it, I don't care what other people think" She added.

"I know that's right Si. Forget anybody who has a problem with you being my little baby who listens forever" Amora said smiling at her sister.

"Sooo Ms. A I have another personal question" Monae said.

"Oh god! What's that Monae?" Amora asked hesistantly.

"Are you still a carpet muncher?" Monae asked causing everyone to burst into laughter.

"Girl your mouth is ridiculous" Amora said to her in between laughing. "But to answer your question, I still find women very attractive but no I no longer munch on their carpets as you call it" She added.

"That's good because you are way too pretty to be around here messing with girl" Monae replied.

"What does me being pretty have to do with my sexual preference?" Amora asked her.

"Nothing but don't you want a family? Husband with kids and all of that good stuff? That's the type of life you deserve" Monae said.

"I deserve to be happy. I conquered making myself happy now whoever I end up with will have to be able to add to what I already give myself. And whatever form that type of love may come in I am open to receive it. Whether it be male or female" Amora explained to her.

"Ms. Amora I want to be just like you when I grow up" Sierra told her.

"Girl I tell her that all the time. Minus the liking girls part. You can keep that far away from me because chicks are crazy" Sionni admitted causing Monae to slap fives with her.

"Sionni what do I tell you every time you say that to me?" Amora asked her.

"To aim to be a better version of myself and never like anyone else" Sionni replied causing Amora to smile.

"Exactly" Amora replied.

"Wait where did Ms. Samantha disappear to?" Monae asked looking around.

"She probably snuck off to talk to her husband. I'm tired so I'm getting ready to call it a night" Amora yawned as she stood to her feet.

"Yes! Cuddle time!" Sionni said with excitement.

"Can we join this cuddle session? Don't leave us out" Sierra whined.

"Yeah come on! I do have one rule though" Amora told them as she stopped walking and turned to face them.

"You cannot touch her with your feet" Sionni said beating her to it. "She will snap out if you rub your feet on her" Sionni laughed.

"I will forget who you are in split second and kick you off that bed so fast" Amora told them seriously looking at Monae specifically.

"Why you looking at me?" Monae asked smiling.

"Because you like trying me" Amora said as she smiled and rolled her eyes.

"Don't be like that Ms. A I'm not going to touch you with my feet! Relax" Monae said to Amora as they all got comfortable in the bed with Amora planted in the middle.

"Amora I love you" Sionni said as she closed her eyes trying to find her sleep.

"I love you too Si" Amora told her.

"We love you Ms. Amora too" Sierra said.

"Yup all that, all that" Monae added causing Amora to laugh.

"I love yall too, now get some rest" Amora told them as sleep found her peacefully.

The remaining days leading up to Mrs. Gionna's home going service were filled with more reminiscing and laughter. Amora began to do exactly what Mrs. Gionna asked her to do which was to celebrate the life she lived instead of mourning her absence. It was the night before the funeral and Amora found herself alone in Mrs. Gionna's room. She had the urge to look through old pictures of Mrs. Gionna and herself so she searched for their old photo album. After finally locating the photo album, Amora got comfortable in the middle of the bed and began to flip through the many pages of pictures. Her eyes fell on the picture she and Mrs. Gionna took on the day she closed on her office building in Atlanta.

"I am so proud of you Amora, but it doesn't end here this only the beginning of the greatness God has in stored for you" Mrs. Gionna said as she looked Amora in her face.

"Why do you always say that Gi? He has already done more than I deserve how can it get better?" Amora asked.

"You will see baby this is nothing compared to what he is going to do with your life" Mrs. Gionna assured her.

Wiping the tears that stained her face, Amora smiled as she continued to flip through the photo album. As she turned to the last page of picture, Amora noticed there was a letter taped to the back cover. Opening the letter Amora began to read as tears began to fall again.

Hey my sweet baby,

I know you didn't think those were my final words to you. I knew you would eventually find yourself looking through these old pictures, reminiscing on the many memories these picture possess from all of our great times together. Amora I want you to use those memories to keep going baby this world needs everything you have to offer. Don't lose your shine mourning me because I am still with you. I did not leave you. Those young girls in your program need your guidance. The same way you needed me and I was there even before you knew you needed me, is the same way you have to be there for them. Take your program worldwide and help and make an impact on as many girls as you can. Every girl needs to know the power they possess deep down inside of them! Create that movement we've always talked about and united women across the world. The power we hold together is better than the power we hold individually. Take over baby and show the love of God through everything you decided to do. I love you Amora and I am with you always.

Love Gi

Amora smiled as she read Mrs. Gionna's letter to her and made a promise that she would do exactly what was asked of her. And she planned to start tomorrow with her speech at the funeral.

The next day..

"Anyone who knows Mrs. Gionna knows she did not play when it came to this young lady who is about to take the mic" Pastor Carter began. "She cracked me in my head with her cane when I first introduced myself to her because she said I made her sweet pea cry" He added causing the entire crowd to laugh. "After seeing how she was with Amora, I wanted her to be my Gi" He said laughing. "Amora are you ready?" He asked causing Amora to nod then walk up to the pulpit.

"Hello everybody" Amora spoke as she cleared her voice. "I'm going to be honest with you guys, I was not prepared for this. Once Gi became such an important part of my life, I never thought about life without her. I just knew I would have forever with her, but that was unfortunately cut short. At first I was angry with Gi because I felt like she should have told me she was sick but as I sat and thought about it, I probably would have made it worse and stressed her out because of my fear and worry and she knew it. Anyone who was blessed enough to have a woman like Mrs. Gionna in their life knows she was something special. Crazy as I don't know what, but full of so much love. I could never thank God or her enough for being able to experience the type of love she offered that was unmatched. Gi instilled so much in me one being the importance of never allowing what someone does to you to change you as a person. She showed me how to pray and leave everything with God. She helped me understand that life happens to all of us and it is up to us to learn and grow from it. Not to become angry, not to become bitter, not to become hateful but to take those bad experiences and search for the lesson inside of them and grow for the better. Never become who may have hurt you and never allow that past hurt to stop you from prospering in the future. Gi you are missed so much words can never describe it nor this feeling of emptiness but I know that with God and time everything will get easier. I just want to encourage someone who may be currently hurting or dealing with a horrible situation outside of their control to seek God. He will give you peace if you allow him to, I promise. It may not seem like it right now, but bad times do not last and if God put you through it please believe me when I tell you that he intends to bring you through it. Thank you" Amora said as she finished her speech then walked back to her seat. Amora smiled and wiped the tears that escaped her eyes as Sionni reached over to embrace her while Sam, Sierra and Monae all smiled at her. Amora wasn't sure how she was going to get past Mrs. Gionna's death but the thing she was certain about was that God would carry her every step of the way. This would be the first time as an adult that she embarked on a journey by herself without the guidance and physical support of Mrs. Gionna but she made a promise to her favorite girl that she intend to keep and that's to keep going! No matter what life may throw her way she will pray on it, leave her worries with God and trust that he will equip her with the necessities to claim her victory. This isn't the last you will hear of Amora so stay Tuned! "From effected to Effective: Amora's Reign" Coming in 2019.

Additional words from Amora.....

Mrs. Gionna death was the hardest things I've ever had to deal with since the incident with Damion and my mother. It was the first time since Gi came into my life that I had that feeling of abonnement again. However the tools and principles she instilled in me reminded me of where I now need to turn. I have a mission in life and that's to show people that you do not have to become who hurt you and the only way for you to ensure that is to forgive those that caused you any hurt. Forgive them for your peace, progression and elevation. When you harbor those ill feelings you give other people power over your happiness, over your peace , over your elevation but when you release that hurt and forgive them you take control and make room for God to pour blessing into your life. I plan to be what Gi was to me to every girl I mentor so that they know the power they possess and collectively we can rise and walk in our full purpose. Don't think for a second that my life is now all glitz and glamour because it isn't however through all of these battles that I still currently face I claim my victory because trouble does not last always. Stay tuned for how I will Reign over everything the enemy thought he stole from me.

Jakeera Mckendrick